THE POLTER-GHOST PROBLEM

ALSO BY BETSY UHRIG

Double the Danger and Zero Zucchini
Welcome to Dweeb Club

THE POLTER-GHOST PROBLEM

BETSY UHRIG

MARGARET K. McELDERRY BOOKS

NEW YORK   LONDON   TORONTO   SYDNEY   NEW DELHI

MARGARET K. McELDERRY BOOKS
An imprint of Simon & Schuster Children's Publishing Division
1230 Avenue of the Americas, New York, New York 10020

For information about special discounts for bulk purchases, please contact Simon & Schuster Special Sales at 1-866-506-1949 or
business@simonandschuster.com.
The Simon & Schuster Speakers Bureau can bring authors to your live event. For more information or to book an event, contact the Simon & Schuster Speakers Bureau at 1-866-248-3049 or visit our website at
www.simonspeakers.com.
Interior design by Jacquelynne Hudson
The text for this book was set in Minister Std.
Manufactured in the United States of America
0123 FFG

2 4 6 8 10 9 7 5 3
Library of Congress Cataloging-in-Publication Data
Names: Uhrig, Betsy, author.
Title: The polter-ghost problem / Betsy Uhrig.
Description: First edition. | New York : Margaret K. McElderry Books, [2022] | Audience: Ages 8–12. | Audience: Grades 4–6. | Summary: Best friends Aldo, Pen, and Jasper stumble onto an abandoned orphanage and discover that freeing a houseful of imprisoned ghosts from an angry poltergeist could get them into serious trouble.
Identifiers: LCCN 2022005709 (print) | LCCN 2022005710 (ebook) | ISBN 9781665916103 (hardcover) | ISBN 9781665916127 (ebook)
Subjects: CYAC: Ghosts—Fiction. | Poltergeists—Fiction. | Orphans—Fiction. | Haunted places—Fiction. | LCGFT: Novels.
Classification: LCC PZ7.1.U3 Po 2022 (print) | LCC PZ7.1.U3 (ebook) | DDC [Fic]—dc23
LC record available at https://lccn.loc.gov/2022005709
LC ebook record available at https://lccn.loc.gov/2022005710

FOR C AND C, WHO GOT ME STARTED

THE POLTER-GHOST PROBLEM

1

THE HEDGE WAS AS TALL AS the three of us standing on each other's heads. It was also thick and prickly, with the kind of needles that would definitely poke at least one eye if we tried to push our way through the branches. The hedge was growing around a rusty iron fence topped with the kind of spikes that would definitely rip our pants and our underpants if we tried to climb over it. And that was if we were lucky.

We didn't want to picture what would happen if we weren't lucky trying to climb over those spikes.

There didn't seem to be any way past the hedge. Which was frustrating and also confusing. Because all three of us had just seen the strange kid we'd been following pass straight through it, backward, with no trouble. This made the strange kid seem even stranger. And it made us even more curious about what was behind that hedge.

Pen and Jasper, who don't agree on much, both think we should keep moving ahead with the action now so the story will be exciting. But I feel like we need some background about ourselves first so the story will make better sense. And since I'm the one typing, even though all three of us are narrating, I get to decide.

Pen and Jasper read this and told me I don't get to decide and to take the background part out. I said I would, but I didn't. I'm counting on them not rereading and noticing I left it in.

So here's a minimal amount of information about us, some of which probably won't come as a surprise.

There were—and are—three of us: Pen, whose full name is Pen Q. (he swears we'll never know what it stands for) Blaisewell; Jasper, whose full name is Jasper Yi; and me, Aldo Pfefferkuchen (the *P* is silent). We've lived in the town of Frog Lake all our lives, and we (obviously) go to Frog Lake Middle School.

Pen and Jasper have known each other since they were in pre-K together. Pen says Jasper attacked him with a plastic shovel on the first day. Jasper says Pen is mistaken. But Jasper says that a lot. My guess is that Jasper was provoked, which is actually pretty easy to do, so I can see both sides of that argument.

Pen and I met at the Frog Lake Kids' Drama Fest the summer after second grade. My parents were hoping it would make me more outgoing, and Pen's were probably hoping it would make him less outgoing. Pen was a huge hit as the talking candelabra in our musical. I was fourth fork from the left.

When Pen introduced me to Jasper, Jasper thought I was annoying at first. And then for a while after that. But I wore him down eventually.

At this point, Pen, Jasper, and I have been friends long enough to know exactly how to get on each other's nerves—and also exactly when to get quickly back off them. This is the basis of our lasting friendship.

And that's all you need to know about us for now.

2

WE FIRST SAW AND FOLLOWED THE strange kid who could pass through prickly hedges and tall spiky fences in the middle of July. Pen was back from vacationing in Maine, and Jasper had a sprained wrist and couldn't go to basketball camp, so there we were, bored and getting boreder.

Jasper says "boreder" isn't a word and we can't use it, but Pen and I have overruled him. Pen and I think that if it isn't a word, it should be.

Anyway, we couldn't skateboard because of Jasper's wrist, so we decided to go to the lake. Unfortunately, my revolting older brother, Neil, refused to drive us there because he was "busy" doing nothing, so we walked to the soccer field instead.

On the way, I asked the others what they were writing about for their Frog Lake Middle School summer journals. I hadn't started mine, I still had no idea what I was going to write about, and I was starting to worry. Our English teacher for the coming fall, Ms. Pilcrow, was rumored to be able to tell immediately if you had written your whole summer journal the day before school started—and grade accordingly.

"I'm doing our trip to Maine," said Pen. "There's so much to work with. Pine needles, ocean, rocks . . . lots of rocks. Nature description–type stuff. I've heard Ms. Pilcrow is a sucker for nature description."

"I'm writing about overcoming my wrist injury," said Jasper. "It's going to be a story of triumph in the face of adversity. Ms. Pilcrow is going to be in tears by the end."

"But you haven't overcome your injury," Pen pointed out. "You're here with us because it hasn't been overcome."

"Yet," said Jasper. "It hasn't been overcome *yet*."

Great. Pen and Jasper were well underway with their teacher-catnip journals, and my summer so far had consisted of fighting with Neil and scratching mosquito bites.

When we got to the soccer field, we spent some time kicking the ball around and complaining about the heat and my troll-faced brother and the fact that no one had thought to bring water. We were sitting on the ground, arguing about whether we could suck moisture out of the grass and whether the chemicals that made it green would poison us if we tried, when we noticed the kid. He was standing at the edge of the field, where it met the woods. He had his hands in his pockets, and he was staring at us.

Several things about this kid were strange. We're going to describe them as if we noticed them right away, even though we didn't. First, he had a bad haircut. It looked like someone had chopped his hair off quickly with dull scissors while he squirmed and tried to get away from them. Second, he was wearing shorts made of wool, which is just wrong. Third, he was wearing a sweater. It was full of holes, but they weren't there to make it a hot-weather sweater by providing air vents. They were there because it was ratty. Finally, he was wearing the kind of lace-up shoes that no one wears unless they're trick-or-treating as an accountant.

He stared at us, and we stared at him. Then he started slowly backing into the woods.

Jasper, of course, was the one to stand up. He was the one to start walking toward the kid. He was the one who said, "Are you coming or not?" And after that, Pen and I had to go with him, didn't we?

Following the strange boy didn't seem that risky at the time. It wasn't as if we were following some sketchy grown-up into the woods—he was a kid like us. There were three of us and only one of him. And even though my nauseating brother describes all three of us as "helpless little twerps," Jasper's tall, and Pen insists he's "mightier than the sword," and I'm seriously wiry. So the kid, who was skinny and pasty, would be easy to take, if it came to that. Above all else, we were really, really bored. We'd been arguing about chewing grass.

The kid was partway into the woods by the time we got to the spot where he'd been standing, so we plunged in after him. At least it was shady in there. Really shady. As in darkish.

"Do you see him?" Pen asked, tripping over a root.

"Maybe up ahead?" I asked, tripping over a rock. "That gray blob moving away from us?"

We tried to walk faster, but in addition to roots and rocks, there were tangles of pricker bushes and low branches and even some dangling vines in our way. We lost sight of the kid for a few minutes and were about to give up when he appeared again, closer to us than he'd been before.

"Is he waiting for us?" Pen whispered.

"Maybe," said Jasper.

"He's obviously not running away from us," I said. "If he'd wanted to do that, he could easily have lost us by now."

"So, what, he's taunting us?" Jasper said.

Just then, Jasper let go of a branch he'd been holding out of his own way, and it snapped back and smacked Pen in the forehead.

"I would be," I said, mostly to myself.

Whether it was his plan or not, we were definitely closing in on the kid. We'd gotten used to the gloom and could see him more clearly now: the gray of his shorts and the lighter gray of his sweater. The different-size holes in his sweater. The paleness of his skin and hair.

Did we notice at the time that he didn't seem to be walking in the usual way? We can't remember, but we don't think we did. We probably would have said something about it, something like *Why are that kid's arms and legs not moving when he walks?* or *How can that kid move in a straight line through these woods when we keep tripping and getting snagged on thorns and thwacked by branches?*

We didn't ask questions like these, so we must not have noticed. In our defense, we were busy trying to keep up with him in spite of all the tripping and snagging and thwacking.

We have no idea how long we were in the woods. All we know is that eventually the kid broke free of the trees, and maybe thirty seconds later we did too.

The sun was dazzling when we emerged, and it took a while for our eyes to adjust. When they did, we could see the kid standing maybe twenty yards away from us in front of an enormous hedge, the one we've already described. He was facing us, and as we watched him, he slowly raised a hand in a wave or maybe a salute. His skin and clothing had taken on a greenish tinge from the light filtering through the hedge. At least that's what we assumed at the time.

"Let's go over there," said Jasper.

"We can't," I said. I had recognized the carpet of plants between us and the hedge for personal reasons. "We're wearing shorts, and that's poison ivy."

"He's wearing shorts too," said Pen. "Come on—he's waving at us."

"Maybe he's not allergic to poison ivy," I said. "But I am. I'll be itching for weeks."

Jasper was itching to charge across that poison ivy, I knew. And Pen was always up for making a new friend, eerie or not.

"I'm sorry," I said. "I'm letting you guys down."

Pen waved back at the kid and yelled, "Sorry! Poison ivy!" He pointed dramatically at the ground and then made exaggerated scratching motions.

"Stop that!" I hissed.

"I'm trying to be friendly," said Pen.

"You look like a dork," Jasper said.

"Let's tell him we'll come back later," I said.

But by the time we'd discussed all that, the strange kid, still facing us, was moving through the hedge. His greenish form melted into its depths without a hesitation or a sound.

3

WE STOOD ON THE EDGE OF the poison-ivy moat, our mouths hanging open. At least I know my mouth was hanging open, because a bug flew into it.

"How—*ptooey*—did he go through there like that?" I asked, spitting out my bug.

We thought about the possibilities.

Then Pen said, "I'm thinking that hedge is actually a hologram. Either that or the kid is a hologram. Or maybe both."

"Why, exactly," said Jasper in his fake-patient voice, "would there be a hologram of a hedge or a kid or both out here in the middle of nowhere, surrounded by poison ivy?"

"Well," Pen began, taking his time, working on his theory as he spoke, "it's probably a secret government headquarters of some kind, where they invent and test holograms, see if they'll fool people. Ingenious."

I was sort of wondering why, if the government was smart enough to do something as complicated as making holograms, it wasn't smart enough to, I don't know, help poor people more, when Jasper came back with "The government? Really?" Which is kind of what I'd been thinking, only not as wordy.

"Or maybe the army," said Pen. "Maybe this is a top-secret army base where they're making hologram soldiers."

"First," said Jasper, no longer bothering with fake patience, "that kid didn't look like a soldier. And second, the army is still run by the government."

"Is not," said Pen.

"Is too."

"Maybe there's a mad scientist's lab behind that hedge," I said, mainly to stop the bickering. "And he's the one making the holograms."

"A mad scientist? Are you serious?"

"Why not? It makes as much sense as the government."

"The army."

"Whatever."

Our voices were getting so high-pitched that the birds

in nearby trees seemed to think we were talking to them, and they joined the discussion, though we couldn't tell whose side they were on.

The real reason we were getting so worked up, of course, is that all three of us were thinking the same thing, deep down inside, and no one wanted to be the one to say it. It was too ridiculous—way more ridiculous than government / army / mad-scientist holograms.

We let the birds carry on the argument for a while, and then I finally said it. "I don't think that kid was a hologram. I think he was a ghost. And so do you."

No one responded. Even the birds went quiet.

My dad is big on "unspoken agreements," the kind where people agree to do something without having to talk about it. My derelict brother is not a fan, which is a source of tension in the family. Anyway, Pen, Jasper, and I made an unspoken agreement as we stood there at the edge of the woods. And it was to turn around and run. As fast as we could. Away from the hedge and its disappearing kid.

We don't need to go into details about what our run back through the trees and roots and rocks and pricker bushes was like, or who fell down, or who ran headfirst into a tree. We all looked pretty bad by the time we tumbled out of the woods, by sheer luck almost right where we'd started at the edge of the soccer field.

Jasper's hair swoop had toppled, and Pen's head had sprouted twiggy twists. I probably looked like someone had turned me upside down and tried to use me as a rake. We were sweaty and we were panting and we were bleeding, and we still didn't have any water. We flopped down on the grass and sweated and panted and bled for a while. Then we sat up.

"So," I said, pulling burrs off my shorts, "if that kid was a ghost—just assuming, for argument's sake—what was he doing? Did he want us to follow him through that hedge? Or was he messing with us, hoping we'd get poison ivy?"

"You don't really hear about ghosts trying to make people itchy," said Jasper. "That's not something they seem to do."

"There are good ghosts and evil ghosts," said Pen matter-of-factly. "An evil ghost probably wouldn't hesitate to give you poison ivy."

"What are you *talking* about?" said Jasper. But this type of blanket objection didn't work on Pen, and Jasper knew that better than anyone. So he changed course. "Giving someone a rash is such a dopey thing to do," he said. "If I were an evil ghost, I wouldn't lure people into poison-ivy patches. I'd lure them into, like, quicksand. And then I'd hang around laughing while they sank."

"You have a point," I said.

"I don't think that kid was an evil ghost, though," said Pen. "I mean, think about it. He waved at us. That seemed friendly."

"So he's a friendly ghost?" Jasper said. "Is his name Casper?"

"Huh?" said Pen, who wasn't allowed to watch cartoons, even really old ones.

"Picture the kid when we first saw him," I said. "Did he look like he wanted to lure us to some kind of doom, even a dopey one like poison ivy? I don't think so."

Pen was nodding. "He didn't look mean," he said. "He looked . . . sad."

We sat there for a while longer, getting thirstier and still bleeding all over our shirts.

"I could really use some water," I said. "And a few dozen bandages."

"Me too," said Pen. "We should go."

The three of us got up and walked toward the sidewalk.

Jasper kicked a pebble. Hard. We watched as the innocent pebble tumbled down a storm drain. We heard the *plop* as it landed.

"You want to go back," Pen said to him.

"Of course I do," said Jasper. "I have a zillion questions about what we saw. Don't you?"

"Yes," I said, "but we can't rush into this."

Jasper heaved a gigantic sigh and looked for another pebble to victimize.

"We don't want to end up with a repeat of the wasp episode," said Pen.

He was referring to the time we'd found a huge wasp nest attached to the back of Jasper's garage. Jasper had insisted it was empty and made us knock it down with sticks. It wasn't empty.

"*Pff,*" said Jasper.

"Or the ice episode," Pen went on. "Remember when you said that the ice on Frog Lake was totally solid, and we almost drowned?"

"No one almost *drowned*," said Jasper.

"Only because of that guy with the ladder!" said Pen.

"How about this?" said Jasper. "We come back tomorrow, when we're prepared."

No one could argue with that.

MY HOUSE WAS THE FARTHEST FROM the soccer field, and to be honest, as soon as I was alone, I began to feel nervous. Not scared or anything major. Just nervous. Maybe a little creeped out. To be honest again, even though it was hot, I shivered a tiny bit, thinking about the way that kid had *melted* into that hedge.

My grotesque brother was washing the car in the driveway when I got there. This was part of a Written Agreement with our parents, drawn up following his Incident with the Car and the Neighbors' Garden Gnome. Which was hilarious. I thought they were going to need the jaws of life to get that gnome out of the back bumper. There's still a gnome-shaped dent there.

"Hey, Typo," Neil said when he saw me. "What happened to you?"

"What do you mean, what happened to me?"

"Why are you all scratched and bloody? You lose a fight with a preschooler at the playground?"

"Funny," I said. "Maybe if you'd taken us to the lake, I wouldn't look this way."

"Here," he said, "let me clean you off." And he sprayed me with the hose. "There! That's just as cooling as a swim in the lake, right?"

I dripped my way into the kitchen in search of water to drink instead of wear. My mom was in there, as usual. She's a recipe tester, so she spends a lot of time cooking— mostly weird stuff that none of us want to eat.

"What happened to you?" she asked, trying to dry my face with a dish towel that smelled like old food.

"Neil sprayed me with the hose," I said, ducking away from her and her towel.

She sighed. "Why can't you two get along?"

"Because one of us is him," I said.

"How did your shirt get blood on it?" She dabbed at my chest with the towel.

I told her that Pen had had a bloody nose and some of it splattered on me. Pen's nose bled if you even breathed on it, so Mom bought this without questioning. I got myself a giant glass of ice water and went up to my room.

I was still pretty shaken from the possible ghost sighting and also shivering from being soaked with the hose. But as I changed into dry clothes, my nervousness started to change into excitement. Because it occurred to me that a ghost story would make the most amazing summer journal ever. Today alone there had been mystery, terror, even blood—Ms. Pilcrow would be on the edge of her seat! This was some A+ stuff already.

I immediately sat down to type a description of what had happened in the woods while it was fresh in my memory.

I type a lot, as anyone who knows me could tell you. I type so much that my foul brother calls me "Typo." He thinks that's hilarious because a typo is a mistake. A few years ago, I started typing stuff that happened to me on an old tablet of my mom's, mainly in the form of a List of Grievances Against Neil. It became a daily habit, like a diary but with more insults.

Recently, my dad gave me his (swear word, worse swear word) laptop when he got a new one, which has upped my typing game by a lot. Dad hated the old laptop, which is why he always used at least two different swear words to describe it, but it works fine for me because I don't try to play games or search the internet with it. Attempting either of those things would be like taking a tricycle out for a spin on the highway. I just type.

Pen and Jasper came over later that afternoon to plan the next day's ghost investigation. They found me typing the details of the possible sighting and started reading over my shoulder. That's when things got complicated.

"Are you typing about what happened to the three of us?" Jasper asked.

"I'm thinking I can use it for my summer journal," I said.

Which was a mistake.

"But it happened to the three of us," Jasper protested. "You can't use it for your own journal."

"Yeah," Pen echoed. "It belongs to all of us. We own the copyright."

Needless to say, that wasn't accurate.

"But you two already have awesome summer journals," I said. "I've got nothing. I need this."

"My summer journal is not awesome," said Pen.

"What about the nature descriptions?" I asked.

"I got a sunburn, I stubbed my toe on a rock, and I froze my knees off in ice-cold water," said Pen. "End of nature descriptions."

"What about you?" I turned to Jasper. "And your triumph over adversity?"

"What triumph?" Jasper said bitterly. "I'm here, aren't I? Not playing basketball."

"We can't write a summer journal together," I argued.

But it turns out I was wrong about that.

Jasper's mother called Ms. Pilcrow that very evening and got permission for us to work on our summer journal as a group project. We had no idea how she made that happen, but Jasper's mother could be fierce. At first I was relieved. A group project would spread the work among three of us. But then I got a taste of what having coauthors is like.

As soon as he heard we'd gotten the go-ahead, Pen called me. He asked me to stop accurately describing my off-putting brother in *our* journal. He had given it some thought, he said, and he was afraid that Neil might read it and take revenge on all three of us. I wasn't worried about that happening, though. Why? Simple. The last story my noxious brother voluntarily read featured a talking backhoe. Words on the page are like extra-strength Neil repellent. I assured Pen that we were in no danger from him or his revenge.

Jasper called next, to inform me that, in his opinion, I was spending too much time on personal details and smelly towels in *our* journal and slowing the story down.

"We need to focus on the action," he said. "Keep it interesting."

"Teachers love details," I assured him.

This was met with such a long silence that I thought he'd hung up.

"All right," I said. "I'll only put in details we agree on."

"Good," Jasper said. "But I'm not sure why you get to be the 'I' in the journal if it's a group project."

"Do you want to type it?" I asked, knowing he didn't.

"No."

"Okay, then. I'm the 'I' because I would feel ridiculous calling myself 'Aldo.'"

And so it was agreed. The three of us would write a ghost story as our summer journal.

A+, here we come!

5

BY THE NEXT MORNING, MANY MORE phone calls later (no, none of us had cell phones, so we couldn't text, and yes, it is a sore spot, thanks for bringing it up), we had finally agreed on a plan for getting across the poison ivy. Even though it was a warm day, we wore long pants with long socks pulled up on the outside of them. We looked as dorky as you are picturing, maybe dorkier. Fortunately, we didn't see anyone we knew during our raid of the alley behind Billy Buster's ice cream shop, where we pulled three big flattened cone boxes out of the dumpster.

Warning: If you are ever tempted to go near the dumpster of a shop that sells milk-based products in the middle of summer, don't.

Just don't.

In addition to our cone boxes, we each had a small backpack full of supplies. These included water bottles and bandages, plus bandannas to tie around our foreheads in case we got sweaty. This time we were ready for anything.

When we arrived at the soccer field, we argued for a while about whether to wait and see if the kid showed up again or go into the woods ourselves. Then we compromised. We waited for what felt like a long time but was really only seven minutes according to Jasper's watch, then went into the woods.

As soon as we got in there, we realized that we had no idea where to go. We'd been following the kid on the way in yesterday, and following sheer panic on the way out. Neither of these was available to us now. We stood there in the woods, feeling foolish and also hot in our long pants.

In the end, yesterday's sheer panic led the way.

"You know what," said Jasper. "You can actually see where we came through the woods before. Everything is still sort of broken and squashed."

He was right. "It looks like an enraged rhino went trampling through here," I said.

Pen laughed, but not at my awesome simile. "You don't get rhinos in these parts," he said.

"These parts?" said Jasper. "What are you, some kind of ancient mountain man?"

"What's an ancient mountain man?"

"Scraggly beard, hand-whittled pipe, can fix a broken bone using a stick and some moss. Mountain man."

"You know I'm not allowed to whittle anymore," said Pen.

Like trackers, or maybe ancient mountain men (but probably not), we followed the signs of our own blundering through the woods. It took a while, longer than it had following the kid in yesterday, and a lot longer than it had running out, but eventually we made it to the edge of the woods, and the poison ivy, and the hedge.

"There it is," said Jasper.

"Yup. There it is," Pen agreed.

"Is it me or does the whole setup look creepier today?" I asked.

"It's you," said Pen and Jasper at the same time.

But they were lying.

If you were wondering about the ice-cream cone boxes, here's where they come in. What we needed to get across the poison ivy, we figured, was a bridge. Since we didn't have the time or the materials or, let's be honest, the skills to build a real bridge, we decided a temporary cardboard bridge would do. We'd spent enough time at Billy Buster's to be familiar with the flattened cone boxes they put out in the dumpster every day, and it just came together.

Jasper would like to specify that the cone boxes were his idea, and that Pen and I had been thinking small, along the lines of shoeboxes, before he suggested them.

Pen would like to specify that cardboard was his idea, and that Jasper and I had been thinking along the lines of newspaper before he thought of it.

I would like to specify, since specifying seems to be what we're doing, that Pen and Jasper were talking along the lines of somehow getting an industrial-size drum of weed killer and dragging it out here until I came up with the bridge idea.

We threw down the three flattened boxes and walked across two of them, landing on the third. Then, wearing gardening gloves we'd borrowed from our parents without asking, we picked up the ones we'd walked across and threw them down ahead of us. It was way slower than we'd pictured, and we had a hard time staying clumped together on the same box while we picked up the ones behind us and then turned and put them down ahead of us.

When we were about halfway to the hedge, we stopped to drink some water and rest. We must have looked ridiculous. Like an old painting called *Three Chuckleheads in a Poison-Ivy Patch*. But we kept going until we got to the base of the hedge. At least here we could each stand on our own box while we figured out what to do next.

Which turned out to be look at each other and feel foolish. Because we hadn't gotten any further in our planning than making it across the poison ivy. We were so proud of ourselves for coming up with the cone-box bridge idea that we had forgotten about what we would do when we got to the impenetrable-looking hedge.

We all agree that it's a sign of our maturity that we didn't turn on each other and start pointing fingers of blame.

"Where's that handy guy with the ladder now?" I asked.

"There has to be a way in," said Jasper.

"Of course there is," said Pen. "That kid got through yesterday no problem."

"Pen," said Jasper, "one of the main reasons we believe that kid is a ghost is he was able to do that. He was able to do that, we think, because he has no physical body."

"He's non-corporeal," I added.

I'm not proud that I said this. I have a big vocabulary, and sometimes stuff like that just comes out. My dad calls it "verbal diarrhea." I usually try to keep a lid on it, for obvious reasons, but sometimes when I'm under stress, I can't help myself. Hey—it's better than actual diarrhea in those situations.

"Maybe there's an opening in the hedge somewhere," said Pen. "Don't most hedges have openings? They're not closed systems, right?"

This was a good idea, and it made up for Pen's earlier boneheadedness. (I was going to say "thickness" here, and then I changed it to "denseness" before I settled on "bone-headedness." Which made me realize how many words for "not smart" involve having a physical body, which was our problem in the first place. Pen and Jasper have told me to take this whole section in parentheses out because it is a perfect example of acute verbal diarrhea. We'll see if that happens.)

The hedge stretched for a long way in both directions from where we were standing. Then it turned a corner at both ends. We had no idea how far we would have to cone-box-bridge around it, hoping to find an opening. But we weren't going to give up and go home, so we resumed clumping and throwing our boxes without complaint. Mostly.

We don't want to guess how far we would have gone in the wrong direction if we hadn't been interrupted. We probably would have kept going at least until dark. We were that determined. Plus, we'd brought snacks. But we hadn't gone more than a few cone-box rotations in the wrong direction when we heard a voice. It came from inside the hedge, very near to us. It wasn't loud, but we weren't expecting it, so it startled us. A lot. We literally jumped. In fact, Pen jumped right off the box we were clumped on and landed in the poison ivy.

"You're going the wrong way," the voice said.

6

THE VOICE HADN'T SOUNDED LIKE A typical movie or TV ghost. It hadn't said, "You're goooooooing the wroooooong waaaaaaay." But it hadn't sounded like a living-human voice either. It was dry and whispery, as if it hadn't been used much. And it had come from a place inside the hedge that a living person couldn't possibly have been in.

So why, instead of abandoning our cone boxes and running for it and dealing with any poison-ivy rash when we were safe at home, did we stay? And why, on top of staying, did we obey what we were now sure was a ghost voice and turn around and head in the other direction?

Well, we've argued about that. And there are several different theories, some more rational than others. But mostly we think we believed the ghost voice because it sounded like a kid's voice. A kid who didn't speak much. A kid who may have had a sore throat with some phlegm. But still a kid.

It was definitely a creepy situation. But it didn't seem like a *dangerous* situation. At least not at the time.

Anyway, we turned around and started cone-boxing the other way. We passed the spot where we'd started and eventually rounded a corner of the hedge. When we got past that corner, we could see that the hedge was much longer on the sides than it was on what we considered the front. It went on and on until it buried itself in trees. From this angle, we could see that there were trees inside the hedge too. And among the treetops, back away from the front section, was a roof.

"There's a house in there," said Jasper.

"A big house," I said.

"A haunted house," added Pen.

This was what my father calls "stating the obvious," and neither Jasper nor I appreciated it.

"Almost there now," said the ghost voice from, it seemed, inches away. The voice was louder this time.

The three of us jumped again, and one of us let out a little scream. It doesn't matter who.

We kept going. We were all thinking the same thing, we discovered later when we compared thoughts. We were all thinking that yes, the ghost was a kid, and he seemed harmless and even helpful. But what if he lived—if that's the right word, and we don't think it is—in that haunted house with a bunch of unharmless adult ghosts who were making him lure us in so they could . . . Our thoughts branched off here into different but equally horrifying images.

"Here," said the voice, mercifully distracting us from our images.

We stopped.

"Here what?" Pen asked.

Jasper and I are going to admit on the record that we were impressed with Pen for being brave enough to speak to the ghost voice. Although, to be fair, among the three of us, Pen is always the one to speak to strangers.

We waited for a response, wondering as the silence went on if Pen had been somehow rude. What if ghosts, even kid ghosts, were supposed to be called "Your Ghostliness"? The ghost didn't reply, so we examined the hedge at the spot where the voice had said "Here."

"Look," said Jasper. "A hole."

Sure enough, there was a hole through the lowest branches of the hedge, as if a largish animal had tunneled its way through there. (I thought badger; Pen went with wolverine, to which Jasper responded, "I don't think there are wolverines in *these parts*.") The branches had been broken or chewed away, and as we peered in, we could see that the fence was in bad shape. A lot of the rails were crooked or bent, and a few had fallen off right where this tunnel went through the hedge.

"Are we supposed to crawl in there?" I asked.

"I guess so," said Pen.

"Are we going to?" I asked.

"Of course we are," said Jasper. "We didn't come all this way to wimp out."

"Then you go first," I said.

Jasper held up his sprained wrist like a trophy. "I can't," he said. "I'm going to need one of you to pull me from the other side."

"You go first, Aldo," said Pen. "I'll push Jasper through from here."

I got down on my hands and knees and stuck my head into the hole. I could see daylight coming from the other end, but not much more.

"We're right behind you," Jasper offered.

"You better be," I said. Then I lay down on my stomach and wormed my way through the opening.

My backpack got caught on a branch, and I had to wiggle around to get loose. My elbows got scraped, and the front of my shirt will probably never be the same color again, but I made it through. Jasper came behind me, and I pulled on his good arm while Pen made a bunch of pushing noises but actually did nothing helpful.

When we were all on the other side of the hedge, we stood up and surveyed the terrain. (Pen and Jasper agreed to allow those unusual words here because they sound tough and cool, which most unusual words—in their opinion—do not.)

We were on what might at one time have been a lawn. It was now a field of weeds that we could tell was home to a vast population of ticks. Unfortunately, the tunnel was too small to allow the cone boxes through, so it was a good thing we had on our dorky socks-over-pant-legs outfits. There were a few trees scattered around, and sure enough, toward the back of the property was a large house. It had maybe once been a paint color, but now it was the gray of weather-beaten wood. It was three stories tall, with a peaked roof that had some big holes in it. It had a lopsided, unsafe-looking front porch. Its shutters were mostly dangling and some had fallen into the weeds, possibly taking out whole tick clans.

It looked, in other words, in case you need it spelled out, like the classic haunted house.

7

"IS THERE ANY WAY THAT HOUSE could look more haunted?" Jasper asked.

"Maybe if it had some sheets in the shape of people sticking out the windows and yelling 'Boo,'" I said, picturing a Halloween card my great-aunt had sent once.

Maybe we were all picturing something cartoonish and harmless, because Jasper started walking toward the house, and Pen and I followed without questioning the wisdom of doing that.

It was really quiet inside the hedge. Ticks don't make any noise, but there were no other bugs in that field making the usual summer bug sounds. And no birds were chirping or cawing or making any of the other usual bird sounds. All we could hear was the swishing of our own footsteps through the long grass and its ravenous ticks.

As we got close to the house, Jasper said, "That's something you don't usually see with typical haunted houses."

"What?"

"A sign. See that metal signpost near the front steps?"

"Does it say 'Haunted House This Way'?" Pen asked. He had to wear glasses to see the blackboard at school, but he refused to wear them "in real life," as he called not being in class.

"No, it says 'Grauche Orphanage for Orphans,'" Jasper said when he was near enough to read the words under the mildew and rust. "Orphanage for *Orphans*?" he said. "Isn't that kind of repetitive?"

"It does seem like overkill to have it twice," I agreed.

We arrived at the front steps of the haunted house. Which we now knew was actually a haunted orphanage. Which didn't make it any less creepy for anyone.

"So does this mean that the ghost kid we saw was a ghost orphan?" Pen asked.

"That would explain his outfit," I said. Though maybe it wouldn't. What did I know about ghost orphans?

"Watch that broken step," said Jasper, climbing up. "And that one. And that nail sticking out there."

The obstacle course didn't end with the top step. The porch was seriously tilted and missing several important boards. A wooden screen door with only torn remnants of screen was propped against the house. The front door itself was closed, and there were no little windows in it for peering through. There were tall, skinny windows on either side of the door, but there were curtains in them.

"So," I said, "do we go in?"

"It wouldn't be much of an investigation if we didn't," said Jasper.

"We'd have to go home in shame," said Pen.

We pictured ourselves going back through the hedge, back across the poison ivy, back through the woods, back to the soccer field. We pictured ourselves wondering what was inside the haunted orphanage and why the ghost had led us there. We pictured ourselves shrugging, going home, going through the rest of the summer, and going back to school, all without knowing anything more than we knew now.

There was no way.

We weren't leaving without looking inside the haunted orphanage, so we did what any trio of red-blooded middle-school boys would do. We argued about who would open the front door and go in first. Pen lost. As usual. He'd ended up being the first to poke the wasp nest and the first out onto the thin ice as well. What were the odds?

Pen batted away some cobwebs as he approached the door. Then he reached for the door's handle. It was one of those handles that you have to grasp with most of your hand and then use your thumb to press down a thumb-shaped lever on the top. But this one was so big that Pen had to grasp with all of one hand and use most of the other to press down the lever.

The lever moved with a loud click, which sort of surprised us, but when Pen pulled on the handle, the door didn't budge. "I need some help here," he puffed, yanking at the handle, his hair falling in his face and his face turning red.

He had both of his hands on the handle, and there was nothing else on the door to hold on to, so I did the cheesy-comedy thing of grabbing him around the waist and pulling on him.

"You're going to make me puke," he grunted. "Stop that right now."

I did, and Pen let go of the door to get his breath and possibly some of his breakfast back.

"Allow me," said Jasper, who'd been standing on the sidelines watching the cheesy comedy.

"Fine," said Pen. "It's very heavy, though. Or stuck. Or both."

"There's also the possibility," said Jasper, grasping the handle and lever with one hand, "that the door opens inward."

Sure enough, as Jasper pushed instead of pulled on

the handle, the door opened inward with a rasp of rusty hinges and a shower of paint flakes, dust, cobwebs, and a couple of those spiders with the long tangly legs.

Jasper let go of the door as it swung open, and we all stood at the threshold and peered inside the house. At first we couldn't see anything in the gloom. An unpleasant smell wafted out, though. It was a combination of stuff that had gotten wet and never really dried and maybe dead mice and definitely mothballs. Lots and lots of mothballs. As the sunlight made its way past the smell and into the house, we could see an entry hall. There was a tall staircase to the right.

"Did anyone bring a flashlight?" Jasper asked.

"It's broad daylight," I said. "Why would anyone have brought a flashlight?"

"I did," Pen said. He tried to hand it to Jasper, but Jasper swatted it away.

"You first," Jasper said. "Remember?"

So Pen went in, his flashlight beam roaming across walls covered with equal parts ugly trellis wallpaper and mold, and across carpet with bald spots and mystery stains.

"Leave the door open," said Pen. Like we were chuckleheads.

We stood in the entrance hall, trying to get used to the inadequate light and the way-too-adequate smell. To either side of us were arched entryways leading to larger and darker spaces, and in front of us, past the staircase, the hallway narrowed and kept going, with various closed doors on either side.

"Where to?" asked Pen, moving his flashlight beam across the options.

"Let's start with the room on the left and try to move clockwise around," said Jasper.

This seemed logical. Pen pointed the flashlight to the left.

As soon as he did that, almost as if he'd caused it by poking his light where it didn't belong, there was a crashing sound from deep inside the house. If you heard a noise like that in your own house, you'd assume that whatever your family kept all its breakable dishes in had crashed to the floor. This was followed by a high shrieking sound, like a windstorm. If you heard a noise like that in your own house . . .

Well, you wouldn't. It wasn't an indoor sound.

8

WE FROZE.

If you're thinking we should have turned around and run through that front door and never come back, well, we thought about that. We didn't specifically think about wetting our pants, but that was definitely an option too. Before we did anything else, though, we froze. It's a natural response, the one that comes before "fight or flight." It's the part where you're making up your mind about fighting or flighting. (Jasper was quick to point out that "flighting" isn't a word, but "fleeing" doesn't rhyme, and Pen and I both like a good rhyme.)

The only thing that kept us from running was that the shrieking noise seemed to die down as we stood there in our frozen positions. There were two or three smaller crashes, maybe oversize antique vases being shattered against walls, but they were like aftershocks from the original giant crash. Then the shrieking stopped. The house was quiet except for the sound of three boys whimpering a tiny bit. And who could blame them?

When the quiet had continued for a while and the whimpering stopped, we got up the nerve to inch our way into the big room on the left that was probably once called the parlor. I don't know that for sure (Pen and Jasper say I don't know at all), but it seemed stuffy and old-fashioned and parlorish. There were uncomfortable-looking sofas and chairs. There was a fireplace with a dark wooden mantel. There were spindly little tables everywhere with those tacky little doohickeys my dad calls bric-a-brac all over them (think shepherdesses, and poodles with shaved-ball tails).

As our heart rates went back to near normal and our eyes adjusted to the dimness, Pen turned off the flashlight. We started to make out some details, most of which involved cobwebs and dust.

Then we saw the ghost who had led us here yesterday.

He wasn't quite sitting on one of the chairs at the far end of the room. He was in a sitting position, but he wasn't touching any part of the chair with any part of himself, as far as we could see. He was more like hovering very close to the chair, pretending to sit on it.

He smiled at us, and there was something about the way he smiled combined with the not quite sitting on the chair that gave us the impression that he was silently yelling, *Look normal, look normal!* to himself as he tried to act casual and welcoming. And then he said, "Welcome," in his whispery voice, and that didn't help his cause one bit.

We were already thinking that maybe we'd investigated enough. We were already starting to edge out of the room. And that's when he added, still with that strained smile, "Do you want to *play*?"

We don't think we would have been more freaked out at that moment if he'd morphed into a fire-and-snot-spewing demon and done the *mwah-ha-ha-ha-haaa* laugh and asked us if we wanted to roast in a pit of doom. "Play"? Really? How old did we look to him? And how old was he? Even if he was a ghost, he should have understood that all of us were too old to be talking about playing.

"*No,*" said Pen in the tone of voice you'd use if someone asked if you wanted to roll in wet garbage. And again, Jasper and I have got to hand it to Pen for answering the ghost.

"I have some matches here," said the kid, his desperate smile widening disturbingly. "We could play with matches." He pointed at the spindly table nearest to his chair, and sure enough, there was a big box of kitchen matches on it.

"Why would we want to play with matches?" Pen asked.

At this point, Jasper and I decided Pen would be our spokesperson. He was doing pretty well, and neither of us was at all comfortable talking to someone who could hover over a chair like that.

"Isn't it fun?" asked the kid. His smile was starting to droop, and a worried expression was replacing it.

"I wouldn't know," said Pen. "I've never played with matches. But it doesn't seem like it would be fun."

"Oh, I'm sure it is," said the kid. "You could maybe light a few small fires and see what happens. . . ."

"I don't think—" Pen started, but Jasper had had enough.

"Are you kidding?" he said. "Play with matches? You think we're going to play with matches in an abandoned house in the middle of nowhere? It's a total cliché. This place would burn down in two seconds with us in it, and we'd be living legends of stupidity. Except not living."

"No offense," put in Pen.

The kid shrugged. "I tried," he said.

"Not very hard," said a voice that didn't belong to any of the four of us. We knew this because it was a girl's voice.

Pen and Jasper and I jerked our heads around, looking for the source of the voice. It was coming from a sofa beside the fireplace. From a girl who hadn't been there before. She was hover-sitting above the sofa, her legs crossed primly. She had long curly red hair and was wearing a shabby dress with a shabbier apron over it. She had on the same kind of lace-up shoes as the boy, only hers looked too big for her. She was maybe a year or two older than us.

"Hello," she said pleasantly. "I'm sorry if I startled you."

"She was there the whole time," the boy put in quickly.

But we were very sure she wasn't.

"Nice of you to visit," the girl said. "Please sit down." She gestured at a sofa opposite the one she wasn't quite sitting on. She didn't seem to notice that none of us moved. "Over there is Theo," she said, cocking her head in the direction of the boy. "He's a good kid, but his manners are a little rusty."

Theo waved half-heartedly at us. "Nice to meet you," he said.

"My name is Franny," said the girl. She uncrossed her legs carefully and sat forward.

The next thing that happened was ultra-weird, but we all saw it and we swear it did happen. She went to rest her forearms on her knees, the way you would if you were trying to have an earnest talk with someone. Only instead of resting on her knees, her forearms *sank into them*. It was strangely fascinating to watch her arms blend with her knees for an instant before she noticed and jerked them upward. Then she tried again, this time positioning her arms a half inch above her knees and holding them there in a way that would make a living person very tired.

She shook her hair away from her face in that pretending-it-didn't-happen way that girls do, then said, "Theo didn't mean to insult your intelligence by suggesting you play with matches. We were hoping you could light some of the candles in here. It's so dark and hard to see."

Pen, bless him, pointed out the obvious. "You could open the curtains," he said. "It's sunny outside. You could see better if they were open."

We're all fairly sure Theo snickered at this, but the girl pretended not to hear him and so did we.

"I suppose you're right," she said. "Perhaps, if it's not too much trouble, you would be so kind as to light a fire in the fireplace, then?" She wrapped her arms around herself without touching anything and shivered. "It's so chilly in here."

Jasper frowned. "It's got to be eighty degrees in here," he said.

The girl let out an annoyed breath and stood up. "Where did you get these kids, Theo?" she asked. "We needed vandals and you got us Boy Scouts."

"I'm sorry I got Boy Scouts, Franny," said Theo.

"We're not Boy Scouts," said Pen. "Anyway, they're called Frog Scouts here in Frog Lake. You start out as a Tadpole Scout and then move up to—"

"They were all I could find," Theo said. "It's not as if

there's a local vandal store where I could pick some up."

"Actually," said Jasper, "the Smart-Mart is where the vandals hang out. In the parking lot. We could tell you how to get there— What? I'm just trying to be helpful," he said when he saw my expression.

Franny shook her head. "Look," she said to the three of us. "We brought you here because we need help. We have a problem and we can't take care of it ourselves."

"What's your problem?" Pen asked.

"This house," said Theo, "is haunted."

9

EVERY KID WE KNOW HAS A "Well, duh" face, and the three of us were making our versions of it.

Why would a ghost have a problem with a house being haunted? If a ghost didn't want a house to be haunted, couldn't they just stop haunting it? It was like a skunk complaining about the smell in here. Unless . . . (and Pen and Jasper say the same thing occurred to them a few seconds after Theo had spoken) . . . unless these ghosts didn't *know* they were ghosts? We think that happened in an old movie. But if they didn't know they were ghosts, then in what way did they think the house was haunted?

Your mind can run through a lot of questions very quickly. So it didn't seem like a whole paragraph of them went by before Jasper managed to come up with "Um, haunted how?"

"We don't know for sure," said Franny. "There's something evil in this house. It has us trapped somehow. We can't leave."

"We were hoping that if we burned the place down, we'd be free," said Theo.

"But we can't burn it down ourselves," added Franny.

"Why not?" asked Pen. "Is it because you're ghosts, and ghosts don't have any substance?"

Jasper and I sat there, frozen, waiting for the results of Pen's rudeness to happen.

"What?" said Theo. "Us? Ghosts? We're normal living kids! Just like the three of you. We've got all kinds of substance. Substance galore!" He was wearing that forced smile again. This kid was a worse liar than Pen, and that's really saying something.

Franny laughed unconvincingly. "What makes you think we're ghosts?" she asked.

"For starters," said Pen, "I can see through your dress."

Franny looked down quickly.

"Not to your underwear," Pen tried to reassure her. "All the way through. I can see the stripes on the sofa through your dress."

We all could, now that he mentioned it.

"Okay, then," said Franny after a moment. "Yes, we are

ghosts. I'm actually glad that's out in the open. I hope we haven't frightened you."

The three of us shook our heads.

"Good," Franny said.

She didn't believe us, and we knew she didn't believe us, and she knew we knew, et cetera. So we moved on.

"You're right," said Theo. "We can't burn the place down ourselves because we have no substance. Or not enough, anyway." As if to prove his point, he stood up and glided over to the sofa where Franny was, passing right through a couple of chairs and a table with a dreadful vase shaped like a goose wearing a kerchief on it.

"It took several of us working together a week to move that box of matches from the kitchen to here," said Franny. "Lighting one is completely beyond us."

"Please," said Theo. "We don't want to be here. We grew up as orphans in this house; we spent the worst years of our lives here. Just light a few fires and run out the door. You won't get hurt, we promise."

Now we felt sorry for the ghosts. But, as Jasper made clear, "We can't burn down a house. It's a crime. Right? There's a word for it, isn't there, Aldo?"

You may have noticed that up until this point in the conversation, I hadn't said anything, in spite of how wordy I am ordinarily. Some boys are shy around girls or teachers or clowns. I turned out to be shy around ghosts. But technically Jasper was asking the question, which broke the ice for me.

"Arson," I said. "It's called arson. And it's definitely a crime."

"We could go to juvie," said Pen, though he admits now that he had no idea what he was talking about.

"Besides," said Jasper to Theo, "when we first saw you, you were at the soccer field. So how can you be trapped here?"

"We're trapped on the orphanage property," said Theo. "Which includes the woods all the way to the edge of the field. That's as far as I could go."

"What happens if you try to go farther?" Jasper asked.

"Awful pain," said Theo. "Not physical pain, since we have no substance. It's almost like it's in our minds. Ever been stung by a wasp?"

We nodded.

"Leaving the property is like trying to get through a wall of wasps stinging your mind."

We cringed.

"And whatever is keeping us here throws tantrums," said Franny. "There's no other way to describe it. You probably heard what happened after you came inside. Windstorms erupt, and objects get thrown around. The flying objects can't injure us, but there's something about the noise that hurts terribly."

I cleared my throat and, for the first time ever, asked a couple of ghosts a question. "Have you been trapped here ever since you . . . um . . ." I was going to say "became ghosts," but Pen got there first with "Died?"

Both ghosts shook their heads.

"No," said Franny. "That's the strange thing. Or one of the strange things. We've only been here since last fall. It's difficult to keep track of time, but we arrived around then. There are twenty-four of us here that we've counted, and none of us can leave."

"But even if we did burn the house down," said Jasper, "wouldn't you still be trapped on the property?"

"That's what I've been trying to tell you, you dang fools," said a new voice.

10

THE NEW VOICE WAS A BOY'S, and it was coming from somewhere over the mantel.

He appeared gradually, transforming from sort of a
scribbled sketch to a watercolor painting. He hovered a
few feet above the mantel, not even bothering to pretend
to be on a piece of furniture. He seemed younger than
Theo and had a square face and dark, seriously messy hair.
Otherwise he had the same underfed, badly clothed look
as the others.

"Listen to these kids, Franny," he said. "They're pretty
logical for being so young."

Pen, whose parents are constantly telling him he's too
young to play certain video games or see certain movies or

ride certain roller coasters, took automatic offense at this.

"We're older than you are," he said to the new boy.

The boy laughed. "Kid," he said, "don't let our youthful looks fool you. What year is it?"

Jasper told him.

"What month?"

"July."

"Then I'm coming up on my hundred and tenth birthday," said the boy. He laughed again. "And I don't look a day over ten, do I?"

"You died a hundred years ago?" asked Jasper.

The boy laughed again. He sure seemed to be having a good time at our expense. "Lord, no," he said. "I lived to the ripe old age of eighty-nine before I kicked the bucket."

Now we were confused. General ghost knowledge, which we all had at least some of, told us that ghosts looked the way they did when they died. We'd been assuming that a ghost who looked like a kid had to be the ghost of someone who died young. My personal theory until that moment had been that some old-fashioned group tragedy had happened to these orphans—maybe a picnic outing gone horribly wrong.

"You didn't die when you were a kid?" Pen asked for all of us.

"Nope," said the younger (but still really old) ghost. "How old were you when you died, Franny?" he asked.

"Ninety-two," she said. "I *know* I had the right of way in that intersection."

"I was seventy-seven," said Theo. "Out on my boat, fishing. Must have had a heart attack." He sighed. "It was a beautiful day, as I recall."

"So why do you look like kids?" Jasper asked.

"Good question," said Theo. "See, Franny? I didn't do so bad. I got three smart kids. Maybe even smart enough to help us get out of here."

"Should we tell them the whole story?" the younger ghost asked.

"Why not?" said Franny.

The three of us removed our packs and sat down on a scratchy sofa across from the one Franny and Theo were hovering above.

Then we settled in and waited to hear a ghost story.

"It all started about a year ago," Theo began.

"No, it didn't," Franny interrupted. "If we're going to tell them the whole story, we need to begin at the beginning. It all started more than a century ago," she said, "when this house was an orphanage, owned and operated by the Grauches, Pritchard and Ermaline—"

She didn't get any further than that. A huge clanging noise drowned her out. It came from the back of the house at first. The sound reverberated as if someone had thrown an iron vat onto a stone floor and let it roll around while also hitting it with a giant metal spoon.

All three ghosts tried to put their hands over their ears, but their hands pressed into their skulls, which would have been an interesting special effect if any of us had been in the mood for something like that. But we weren't, because now it sounded like the vat was rolling toward the parlor, somehow getting bigger as it came.

Then the clanging noise seemed to have found a friend, as the shrieky wind joined it, and both of them were roaring toward us at the same time.

"Maybe you kids better go!" Franny shouted over the din.

We stood up and put on our backpacks. But the shrieky wind and the clanging were in the room with us now. Our hair blew straight up. Dust and cobwebs whirled around in clouds, and we had to squint to keep the grit out of our eyes. Then the bric-a-brac on the spindly tables started to fly around, banging to the floor and smashing against the walls. The goose vase shattered against the fireplace. The spindly tables themselves fell over and started sliding around as if the whole house were tilting one way and then another. Maybe it was.

"Run!" Theo yelled as the three ghosts faded from sight amid the chaos of noise and airborne tacky decor.

We tried, but the double doors leading from the parlor

to the front hall slammed shut the moment we turned toward them. Pen grabbed a knob and yanked. Then he kicked at the door, then he pounded on it with his fists, then he butted his shoulder against it, but the door failed to open or splinter into pieces.

We ran the other way, toward a doorway at the far side of the room. There was no door there to slam shut, so we darted through, but the wind followed us, grabbing at our hair and our clothes. The bric-a-brac from the parlor followed us too, whacking us as we ran down a dark hallway, frantically searching for a way out.

"Leave us alone!" Pen shouted.

Something hit him in the back of the head, but luckily it was the matchbox. If it had been one of the china cherub candlesticks, he might have gotten a concussion. As it was, he got angry.

"Stop bothering us and we'll leave!" he yelled. "Isn't that what you want?"

Not only would Pen speak up to ghosts, but he would also go ahead and yell at hostile stuff-throwing whirlwinds. So hats off to Pen, once again.

But the evil thing—we'll call it an entity—would not listen to reason. Or maybe it couldn't hear reason over its own noise. It continued to shriek and clang and whirl and chuck stuff at us, and the stuff was getting bigger and more painful. One of the spindly tables caught me in the region of the lower back / upper leg, shall we say. (Yes, it left a mark.)

I myself was ready to admit defeat and curl up in a fetal ball and try to protect my head, the way you're supposed to do if you're attacked by a bear. Jasper grabbed the table that had caused my injury with his good hand and tried to use it as a shield. But it was ripped away from him and crashed into a wall. Today's furniture would have splintered, but this old table, delicate as it looked, bounced off the wall intact and managed to hit Pen in the lip. (Yes, it bled. A lot.)

All seemed lost, and then it started to seem even more lost. A large, blobby figure was lurching down the hall toward us, waving its arms and shouting things we couldn't hear but didn't think we'd like. As it got closer, we saw that it was some kind of hideous Franken-thing.

The Franken-thing was taller than Jasper, but that might have been because its head was so elongated. It was lumpy all over, with skinny arms that seemed to have more than one elbow each, and gangly legs with multiple knees, and at least three different colors and textures of hair tufting out of its misshapen head.

As for its face—well, I am something of an expert on ugliness, living with Neil, but this was beyond human-level ugly and into the realm of alien-life-form ugly. The bulging eyes were practically on top of each other, the bulbous nose looked like it had been stung by an entire flotilla of jellyfish, and the mouth was working away as if it had a huge wad of gum in it.

The thing stopped directly in front of us, still trying to say something. Then it reached for us with its freakishly long arms.

All three of us screamed, and you would have too.

FLYING BRIC-A-BRAC STARTED BOUNCING OFF THE creature, but it kept coming for us, its outstretched arms making it look even more like Frankenstein. (Or Frankenstein's monster, technically. Pen and Jasper can fuss all they want about me being a nerdy egghead show-off, but I think that's worth clarifying even in this terrifying situation.)

The three of us ducked as the thing lunged at us, but it didn't stop to grab us. Instead it dodged around us. Then it turned and windmilled its arms and yelled again.

"True da chicken an ouda doah," it cried.

Or that's what it sounded like, what with the shrieking and clanging and its apparent gum wad–filled mouth.

"True what chicken?" Pen called back.

"Don't engage with it," I told him. "Let's run now that it's blocking most of the stuff."

The creature's head was wagging back and forth like it was going to topple off its neck. "Wun," it said.

"Won what? What did the chicken win?" Pen asked, but Jasper and I were pushing him down the hallway and through a swinging door at the end.

It was quieter once we got through the door. We were in a big kitchen full of old-fashioned appliances and smashed dishes. We didn't stop to investigate, though. We charged toward the daylight at the far side of the room, which was coming from the window in the back door.

We struggled with the door until we realized it was bolted on the inside. Then we struggled with the bolt. Then we practically fell out the door and down the rickety steps and into the long grass.

Jasper had reinjured his bad wrist, and Pen's lip was gushing blood, so it was up to me to ignore my lower-body pain and dash back up the steps to close the door so the Franken-thing and the evil entity couldn't come barreling through to finish what they'd started. Whatever that was. Because their motives weren't clear. Did they want us out of the house, or in it and badly hurt? The signals had been contradictory.

We could still hear noise from inside the house, but it didn't get any louder, so we figured we were safe out here for the moment. Except from ticks. We got our breath and tried to calm down and fished around in our backpacks for tissues to press against Pen's lip. We drank some water. We swabbed water on Pen's face to wash off the blood but mostly smeared it around.

"Let's get out of here," Jasper said, summing up the situation for all three of us.

We made our way around the overgrown yard, staying as far from the house as possible, until we got to the opening in the hedge. One by one, we crawled through the hedge. Once through the hedge, we clumped back onto our waiting cone boxes.

We were tired and scared and bruised and bloody, and the last thing we wanted to do was carefully cone-box our way back to the front of the hedge and the woods beyond.

That's not quite right. The *last* thing we wanted to do was go anywhere near that haunted orphanage again.

We don't know how long we would have stood out there, waiting for the energy to finish getting the heck away from that place. Before we did, the younger ghost, whose name we still didn't know, drifted through the hedge.

"You guys all right?" he asked.

We nodded.

"I'm sorry it went haywire," he said. "Whatever it is that's haunting the orphanage goes off like that sometimes.

Franny and the others, they were really brave coming to your rescue."

"What are you talking about?" asked Pen. "First that noisy wind attacks us, and then some mutant zombie thing yelled at us about winning chickens. No one came to our rescue; we barely got away with our lives."

The ghost laughed. Then he said, "You kids and your mutant zombies. Too many video games and not enough sunshine and exercise. That 'thing,' as you call it, got between you and the attacker. It was telling you to *run*. Through the *kitchen*. It saved your bacon."

"Huh?" we said.

More laughing. "Franny, Theo, and Lorna, I think it was. Charlie might have been in there too. That 'thing' was them, all layered on top of each other. That's the only way we can work up enough substance to do anything physical—we have to bond like that. It's not pretty, I admit, but it got the job done. Did you see that stuff bouncing off them? When we layer up, we become more solid."

"That . . . thing was three different people?" Jasper asked.

The ghost nodded. "At least."

"Which explains the extra knees and elbows," Jasper said.

"Are they okay?" Pen asked. "They got hit with even more stuff than we did, and we're wrecks."

The ghost chuckled. "They're fine. It doesn't hurt to get hit like that, though they do get knocked around some. We haven't really been introduced," he said. "My name's Denny."

"Pen, Jasper, and Aldo," Pen said, pointing us out.

It would have been interesting to shake the ghost's hand, or try to, but Denny didn't offer.

"Nice to officially meet you," he said.

"We should get going," I said. "It'll take us a while to get across this poison ivy again."

"Poison ivy?" said Denny. "Where?"

"All over the place," I said. "That's why we have our socks pulled up over our pants."

Denny didn't laugh outright this time. He just got an expression on his face like he was trying hard not to. "I was wondering about that," he said. "I mean, I may have died of old age decades ago, but I still know dorky when I see it."

"Not dorky. Practical," said Pen.

"Whatever you say," said Denny. "But that's not poison ivy. I was a landscaper, so I know."

"But leaves of three," I said.

"Not all leaves of three are poison ivy," said Denny.

We were already pulling our pants out of our socks.

"So," said Denny when we were done, "are you coming back? We really do need help."

"What about the angry haunty shrieky thing?" Pen asked.

"That is a problem, I'll admit," Denny said. "But we'll do our best to protect you."

"Maybe if we stayed out on the porch?" Jasper suggested.

"That might do the trick," said Denny.

"We could wear helmets," Pen offered. "And shin pads."

"Whatever makes you comfortable," said Denny, not hiding a smirk.

"We'll think about it," I said.

But I'm not sure I meant it.

12

WE WERE SILENT AND SHAKEN AS we found our way back through the woods to the field. We were still kind of clumping even though we didn't need to anymore.

Ghosts were real. We had met actual ghosts. There had been formal introductions. We (mostly Pen) had talked to *actual ghosts*. Which kind of changes everything, doesn't it? Opens a lot of doors in the imagination that lead to places you don't necessarily want to explore. None of us wanted to think too hard about those doors and what lay beyond them in case it interfered with our sleep for the rest of our lives.

I, for one, can only take so much silence when I'm freaked out, though. So when we left the haunted woods and stepped back onto the normal, overly green grass of the soccer field, I opened with: "So. That happened."

"It really did," said Jasper.

"They seemed nice, though, didn't they?" said Pen. "As ghosts go?"

Pen had no idea how ghosts went, but Jasper and I were in no position to nitpick. We were concentrating on not running around screaming, *"Ghosts! Ghosts!"*

"Except for the thing that attacked us," said Jasper. "That didn't seem so nice."

"That one seemed to have a totally different agenda," I agreed.

"Like I said earlier," said Pen, "there are good ghosts and there are evil ghosts. You have to keep them straight or it will mess with your mind."

Our minds were already a mess, but Pen's matter-of-fact attitude was kind of helping, so Jasper and I let him continue.

"We need to help the nice ghosts escape from the evil one," Pen said. "Obviously. We may not be Frog Scouts, but we believe in helping those in need, right? Even if we can see through them?"

We thought about this for a while in silence.

We did want to help the nice ghosts. It was the right thing to do. Plus, we didn't have anything else going on. Plus, stopping now would have meant a crummy ending to our summer journal. B-minus at best.

"If we want to help them, we need to do some research," I said finally.

I liked this idea a lot. Research was normal. Verging on dull. It would be a calming thing to do after finding out that ghosts are real and having to wonder about whether those noises your dad insists are "the heat coming up" are actually something haunting the radiators.

"Research?" Pen groaned. "How is it that you can take the wildest, most exciting thing that's ever happened to us and make it into an assignment?"

"Research about the orphanage and those people who owned it—the Grauches," I said. "We need background information. It might help us figure out what's keeping the ghosts there."

"Background information?" said Jasper in the same tone that Pen had used a few lines up. "What could *be* more fun."

But the research had to wait until all three of us had gone to the urgent care clinic.

I managed to sneak into the house and wash up and change my clothes before anyone saw me, but my mom noticed that I didn't want to sit down to eat lunch (due to my lower-back / upper-leg injury), and she wouldn't let up about it.

"I slept on it funny, that's all," I said, but she didn't believe me.

She called the doctor, and the doctor said to go in for an X-ray.

Pen and Jasper were in the waiting area when we got there.

"My mom thinks I resprained my wrist," said Jasper.

"Mine thinks my lip needs stitches," said Pen from behind a huge hospital-issue ice pack.

"What have you three been doing?" my mom asked the wounded.

"Have you been fighting?" Jasper's mom asked.

"Are you being bullied?" Pen's mom put in.

"Nobody is bullying us," I said. This was the truth only because the word "body" was in there. If I'd said "No evil entity is bullying us," it would have been a lie.

"We were playing football," said Pen, not as concerned about lying as I was. He was trying to make us seem tough and fun-loving, but the mothers were having none of it.

"Of all the nonsensical—" (mine)

"You can't play football with a sprained wrist!" (Jasper's)

"You can't play football!" (Pen's)

One by one, we were called in and X-rayed and bandaged and stitched and lectured. The mothers hung out in the waiting area and talked while we were being treated, so we ended up together again when we were done.

I asked if the mothers could drop us off at the library

when all the clinic's paperwork was filled out. Which they were glad to do. At least there wouldn't be any football at the library.

Pen and Jasper weren't thrilled about an afternoon of research, as you already know, but they agreed it was better than sitting in our separate homes, nursing our wounds, avoiding questions, and interpreting every little noise with a newfound belief in ghosts.

On a library computer, we looked up the Grauche Orphanage for Orphans and didn't find anything. Then we looked up Grauche alone, which gave us too much. Then Jasper remembered Mrs. Grauche's unusual (to put it kindly) first name: Ermaline. That narrowed it down.

In fact, it led to one major fact and some minor factoids, which appeared on a few websites in slightly different forms. The factoids involved the Grauches being dreadful people. The two had written multiple letters to various newspapers complaining about their taxes going to "undeserving layabouts who are too lazy to be rich" and to public schools "infested by hordes of nose-picking children." Stuff like that.

The major fact was that Mrs. Ermaline Grauche, along with her husband, Mr. Pritchard Grauche, had died more than a century ago when a ship they were on went down in the North Atlantic.

If you're any kind of a disaster nut, like Pen is, you will automatically jump to a conclusion here, but you'd be wrong. They didn't go down on the *Titanic*. Instead, they went down on a cheap knockoff ship called the *Gigantic*, which was sailing from America to England when a fire broke out onboard and it sank.

The crew and all but two of the passengers were rescued in the plentiful lifeboats, but the Grauches went down with the ship because they refused to believe it was sinking. In fact, according to the captain, they refused to leave the auditorium, where they were giving a lecture called "Children's Books—What a Waste of Paper."

The captain told a reporter that when he pointed out the freezing-cold salt water sloshing around their shins, the Grauches claimed he was trying to "sabotage" their lecture. "When I attempted to drag them to safety, they hit me with a fire extinguisher," he said. The captain also told the reporter that he suspected the Grauches themselves had caused the sinking by setting fire to a pile of Beatrix Potter books in some kind of grotesque demonstration.

"They burned the Flopsy Bunnies?" Pen whispered, aghast.

Jasper offered to look at old maps of Frog Lake in the local-history room to see if the orphanage property showed up on them. I decided to go with him, to see if I could find more about the Grauches or the orphanage in any books about town history.

Pen refused to go into the local-history room. He said the librarian there gave him "the heebie-jeebies." Instead, he volunteered to look up the *Gigantic* in some maritime-disaster books he was familiar with.

Jasper was the only one who found anything.

"Here it is," he said, bringing a huge book of old town maps over to where I was sitting. He dropped the heavy volume in front of me with a thunk and pointed to a big plot of land labeled "Grauche."

The librarian jerked her head up from her computer at the sudden noise and gave us the stink eye. She *was* a little daunting. Maybe it was the thick curtain of bangs that hung down to the chunky top frame of her glasses. Or maybe it was the glasses themselves, which were so thick they made her eyes look blurry and all-seeing.

"What happened after they died?" I whispered. "Is there a later map there?"

"Yes. It doesn't say 'Grauche' anymore, though the plot is still there—same size and shape."

"What does it say?"

"Just some initials. 'SPEC.'"

"And what about more recently? Like now?"

Jasper paged through the book. It ended in 1950, so he had to go find the next volume.

"The last book only goes to 2000," he said. "But it still says 'SPEC.'"

We tried looking up "SPEC" on the internet, but if you've tried something similar with a simple set of initials, you understand how that turned out. We now knew that someone or something called SPEC owned the abandoned orphanage, though it was clear they didn't spend any time there, dusting, for example, or weeding, or trimming the hedge.

But by the time we left the library two hours later, we still had no idea who or what they were.

13

PEN CHECKED A BOOK OUT OF the library. It was called *The Big Book of Hauntings: A Comprehensive Guide to Ghosts and Other Specters*. The pictures on the front were cheesy, so we didn't hold out much hope, but it had come from the nonfiction section, so we figured it was worth a try.

We went to Pen's house to see what we could find in the book.

Pen has a weird faith in indexes, it turned out, so the first thing he did was try to look up "shrieky wind, noise of." Shockingly, there was no entry for that.

"Wait," he said. "I'll try 'bric-a-brac, flying.'"

Jasper and I rolled our eyes and waited for that to fail too. Which it did.

Pen was irritated. "How do they get away with calling this book 'comprehensive' if it doesn't have this basic stuff in it?"

He went on to "crashing sounds, loud." No luck. "Tables, being thrown at people." Nope. He really thought he had it with "entities, evil." Nope again.

"This index is totally useless," Pen complained. Which is when he finally let Jasper and me have a look.

"How about this?" said Jasper, running a finger down the column nearest him. "'Destruction, household.'"

"Seriously?" said Pen. "*That's* an entry? Who indexed this book, anyway?"

We ignored that question and turned to page 110.

Which is where we learned about poltergeists.

We're guessing you probably already know what a poltergeist is. In fact, you probably diagnosed the poltergeist problem a while ago, back when we were getting shrieked at and having random junk thrown at us.

But in case you don't know, a poltergeist is an entity you can't see that hangs around a place making noises, breaking things, throwing things, and generally "wreaking havoc," as the book put it. Some people think they are a type of ghost (so dead), and other people think they are caused by a living person who's not necessarily doing it on purpose: Their psychic energy or whatever is tossing things around without their cooperation. Or maybe there are two kinds. "The experts do not agree," according to the book.

Just so you know, Jasper *made* me take out a whole paragraph here on who these poltergeist "experts" are and where they get off calling themselves that when they have so little useful information. Too bad; it was A+ stuff.

"Ah-ha!" said Pen when we'd all huddled around the book and read the poltergeist definition. "It makes sense now."

"What does?" I asked.

"That the entity is a poltergeist. It must have been one of you two"—eyeing me and Jasper—"causing all that chaos. It says here it's often an adolescent that does it. 'Cause of their hormones and excess mental energy."

"It's clear *you're* not dealing with any 'excess mental energy' at the moment," said Jasper.

"What's that supposed to mean?"

"Think about it! The ghosts have been trapped at the orphanage for almost a year. Aldo and I didn't even know it existed until yesterday. How could either of us be the poltergeist?"

"So what is it, then, Mr. Smarty McSmartguy?"

"It's the other kind of poltergeist. The dead kind."

"I haven't gotten to that part yet," said Pen, who didn't always read things in order.

"It was *first*," said Jasper, who did. "Look. It says that a poltergeist can be a malicious spirit haunting a place. That sounds about right, doesn't it?"

It did. Even Pen knew it. We could tell because he didn't say anything. Pen admits defeat by remaining silent.

"Cool," I said, reading ahead. "Look at 'The Case of the Bagpiper of Drumknott.' This house in Scotland has had a poltergeist since the sixteenth century. Everyone who's ever lived there has heard an eerie sound of bagpipes playing in the dead of night, and whenever they try to bake scones, they burn."

"And look at this one, in America," said Jasper. "'The Case of the Authoress of Andover.' This old house has a poltergeist they think is the spirit of a woman who lived there and wrote a book called *Little Ladies* that was a total rip-off of *Little Women* and was never published. Whenever you mention Louisa May Alcott or *Little Women* out loud, china starts getting smashed."

"That sounds familiar," said Pen. "Maybe it was something we said that got that thing so riled up this morning."

"Pen," said Jasper, "I take it back about your lack of mental energy. That actually makes sense."

"What were we saying when it started making all that noise?" Pen asked.

They both looked at me. As the wordy typing guy, apparently I was supposed to remember every syllable that had been spoken that day.

I shrugged, not wanting to immediately live up to their assumption.

They continued to look at me until I cracked.

"Franny had just told us the Grauches' names."

"They are pretty weird," Pen said. "Maybe the poltergeist hates weird names."

"Or maybe it hates the Grauches," I said.

14

WE WERE SITTING ON THE TILTED porch of the orphanage, talking to Franny, Theo, and Denny. Yes, the three of us were sitting around chatting with ghosts, and we're still surprised at how quickly we adjusted to this. I think it boils down to the fact that people are people, no matter what side of the grave they happen to be on. Pen agrees with me. Jasper is shaking his head.

We were wearing our skateboarding pads and helmets. This was a reasonable precaution, since no one wanted to have to explain further injuries to the mothers. Franny nodded approvingly when she saw them. Denny laughed long and hard.

Pen had his library book open in front of us. He was

reading the stuff about poltergeists aloud.

"So if the entity is a poltergeist type of ghost," said Theo, "what type are we?"

We started with the general definition of "ghost" (the index actually included "ghost, definition of," which made Pen's day).

"It says a ghost is 'the visible and often audible manifestation of the spirit of a dead person,'" said Jasper.

"Is that what we are?" said Franny. "Because it doesn't seem right to me. If I were a ghost of my dead self, why do I look like I did when I was fourteen—when I last lived here?"

"I feel the same way," said Denny. "Honestly, I don't think too much about my adulthood lately—which lasted a lot longer than my time here. I feel more and more like the ghost of the Denny who lived at the orphanage."

"Hmm," said Jasper, who'd been reading ahead while they were talking. "Maybe this is it. It says if someone experienced something particularly traumatic somewhere, the manifestation of this memory can haunt the place. It says these hauntings don't necessarily appear as a whole person. It can be a version of a person, or even just clothes or hair or mist or something."

"Ew," said Pen. "I'm glad you guys aren't just hair. Or, like, toenails."

"That does sound more like us," said Franny, ignoring Pen's contribution. "Not traditional ghosts, but something like memory ghosts. Ghosts of the memories and emotions of the kids who lived here."

"Um, I think I might be a traditional ghost?" said a small voice from up near a spiderweb under the porch roof.

Franny's head jerked toward the sound. "Who is that?"

"Um, it's me. Stella," said the voice. "From the orphanage?"

"Stella!" said Franny. "We had no idea you were here. Why didn't you say something?"

"Um, I just did?" said Stella.

She came into view as we watched. A girl of about eight, wearing a dress that should have been frilly and pretty but was tattered and stained. She had long blond hair pulled back by a headband. She looked like the ghost of Alice in Wonderland.

"But you can't be a traditional ghost," said Pen to the new arrival. "You're a kid like the others."

Stella looked down at herself as if to confirm this. "Um, yes," she said. "That's true. But that's all I ever was. I died when I was nine. Here in the orphanage. Of pneumonia, I think."

"I remember," said Franny. "So you've been here . . ."

"All my death," said Stella.

"Are you trapped here like the rest of us?" Denny asked.

"I'm not sure," said Stella. "I've never tried to leave."

Pen was nodding quickly, which was a sign that he was working up to a blurt. Sure enough: "So," he said, still nodding, "there are two different types of ghosts *and* a poltergeist. I think what you've got here"—he was sounding a lot like the exterminator my parents had hired for the flies last spring—"is a major polter-ghost haunting. Get it? Polter-ghost?"

"We got it," said Jasper.

Denny rolled his eyes.

"Has the poltergeist always been here?" Franny asked Stella.

"Um, I don't think so?" said Stella. "I think it arrived around when you all did. At least I never noticed it before you came. But maybe it just took no notice of me."

"Oh, Stella," said Franny. "Were you haunting the place even when the rest of us still lived here?"

"Oh yes," said Stella. "I was so sad when everyone left. Hardly anyone came by after Mr. and Mrs.—"

"Don't say it!" said Jasper. Stella disappeared immediately. "The thing doesn't seem to like that name," he explained to the air where she'd been. "At least that's our theory."

"It's okay, Stella," said Franny gently. "Come back and tell us what happened."

Stella reappeared up by her spiderweb, eyeing Jasper

warily, then floated back down to our level. "After, um, *they* died," she said, "and the rest of you left and the orphanage closed, the only people who came by were from the society. And they only stopped in to clean up and air things out for a few years. Then no one . . ."

"The society?" Jasper said. "What society?"

But Stella didn't seem to want to be questioned by the mean boy who had snapped at her a moment ago. She looked into the distance as if no one had spoken.

"Stella?" Franny prodded.

"Yes, Franny?"

"What society came to clean up?" Franny asked.

"The Society for the Prevention of Encounters with Children."

A tarnished candelabra came crashing through a window and landed heavily on the porch, splintering a board. Stella winked out again. The other ghosts wavered like heat mirages.

It's a good thing Jasper was bent over the book when it happened, because the candelabra had whizzed inches from the top of his helmet, and some pieces of broken window had bounced off it.

"I guess the entity doesn't like that name either," he said more calmly than Pen or I would have.

His tone of voice seemed to steady the ghosts, who firmed up again as he spoke. Except for Stella. She was gone, and I didn't blame her. Imagine speaking for the first time in a century and being snapped at by a mean boy and then having a candelabra thrown at you. (Jasper says if I refer to him as a mean boy again, he's going to give me a real reason for calling him that.)

"Maybe we should use initials from now on instead of names," said Pen. "You know, like 'Mr. and Mrs. G' and—"

"Pen, you are brilliant," said Jasper.

"Huh?"

"Initials," said Jasper. "The society's initials are S-P-E-C. Like the ones on the property map."

15

"WHAT PROPERTY MAP?" SAID FRANNY.

We described the map at the library showing that SPEC owned the former orphanage.

"They must have inherited it from the Gs," said Jasper.

"Sounds like the kind of group that the—ah—Gs would have left this place to, doesn't it?" said Denny.

"Why?" I asked.

"Those two *hated* kids," said Theo.

"*Hated* them," echoed Franny.

"Wait," said Jasper. "They hated kids and chose running an orphanage as a career?"

The ghosts shrugged in unison.

"We worked here like servants," Franny said. "No

school. We weren't allowed to leave the grounds. Harry tried to escape once, I recall. He got his head stuck in the fence, and the Gs left him there overnight. In the rain. To teach him a lesson, they said."

"Tell them about our last names," said Theo.

"Ha," said Denny. "It's almost funny, looking back on it."

"Not really," said Franny bitterly.

"What last names?" Pen said.

"Whenever an orphan arrived," said Denny, "the Gs would give them a first and last name. They said they used the names as a system to keep track of everyone, but it was really another chance to be cruel. Their system," he said, "consisted of giving every orphan a last name that began with the same sound as their first name and rhymed with *ump*."

"And how is that mean?" I asked, without giving it much thought.

"Think about it," said Denny. "My name was Denny . . ."

"Dump," said Pen.

"And Stella Stump and Franny Frump, and so on," said Franny. "I think that explains why I married young—couldn't wait to change my name. To Fickelgruber, no less."

"Not all 'ump' names are bad," said Jasper. "'Jump' is okay."

"Funny," said Theo, "but I don't recall anyone with a name that began with *J*."

"But *tons* of names begin with J," said Pen.

"Poor Roger," said Franny. "He got the worst of it."

"Not to mention me," said a new voice from the porch steps.

"Hey, Charlie," said Theo. "Meet our living friends, Aldo, Jasper, and Pen."

"A pleasure," said a boy who came into view on the second step down. He was tall and had a crewcut with a jaunty cowlick. "I was Charlie Chump," he said, "as you've no doubt already figured out. Nice, huh? The sad thing for me, though, is that my name was really Charlie McCloud, and I wasn't an orphan. I was the paperboy. Mr. G caught me 'snooping around,' as he put it, too close to the hedge, and he kidnapped me and kept me prisoner here."

"Gee whiz," said Denny. "We all thought you were lying about not being an orphan. They told us you were delusional."

"Nope," said Charlie. "I went back to my family right after the ship went down. Boy, was I happy to see them. And they weren't all that great, to be honest."

There was a silence on the porch for a while as the former orphans thought about their time here, and the non-orphans felt a little more grateful for their families— certain brothers excepted, of course.

"You want to see them?" Denny asked us after the while was over.

"See who?"

"The"—his voice dropped—"Gs. Their portraits are hanging in the office inside. Want to go in and have a look? It'll be worth your time, I guarantee."

Theo chuckled. "Did any of you have a big breakfast? Because you don't want to meet them on a full stomach."

"Don't ruin it for them, Theo," said Charlie.

"Okay, okay. I just want them to be prepared."

"What if we disturb the poltergeist again by going inside?" I asked.

"What if we anger it?" Pen added.

"Just keep quiet," said Denny. "And be careful. Stealth mode, got it?"

In stealth mode, we crept inside the house behind Denny. He led us past the staircase, down the dim hallway, and then turned right. Once inside the office, we stood still and waited for any sign that we had bothered the poltergeist. So far so good.

We couldn't see anything in the dark room, so we opened the long, thick curtains. Very quietly. This stirred up a lot of dust, and while that settled, we peered around. Very carefully.

There were two big desks side by side facing the door and some bookshelves behind them with no books. A padded bench sat against the wall between the bookcases—maybe in case one of the Grauches got tired from ordering orphans around and needed a quick lie-down. Tall filing cabinets stood on either side of the door. And, sure enough, hanging on the dark paneled wall opposite the desks were two framed portraits—a man and a woman.

We moved closer to have a good look at the child-hating orphanage owners and bunny-book burners and stubborn shipwreck victims.

Mr. Grauche was thin to the point of skeletal. His suit hung off him like he'd borrowed it from someone twice his size. The bony hand that was visible in the painting resembled something that would grab an unsuspecting teenager in a scary movie. He had a mile-high forehead and mean little eyes. He was making a face—and this was while he was sitting for a portrait—that made it look like he had a grasshopper in his mouth that was trying hard to get out. But he was a catch compared to his wife.

Mrs. Grauche was wearing a fancy dress and loads of clunky jewelry, so she'd clearly made an effort for her portrait. But her lips were pressed together like someone was trying to feed her something disgusting, and her expression implied that something in the room—maybe the painter—smelled terrible. None of which was good. But it was all overshadowed, almost literally, by the eyebrow situation. The woman had *three* eyebrows; there's no other way to describe it.

You know how some people have a little tuft of eyebrow in between their eyebrows? Or they have one sort of continuous eyebrow that goes across their nose? This wasn't like that. Mrs. Grauche had two short eyebrows over the far ends of either eye, and then there was this other eyebrow of equal size and importance right in the center.

You're thinking that this is an easily solved problem to have, but think again. She couldn't shave the center one off—that would have left two freakishly short eyebrows spaced way too far apart. Nor could she have tweezed a space down the middle of the center eyebrow—that would have given her four eyebrows instead of three.

And yes, we have given the whole eyebrow thing a lot of thought. It's what word nerds call a "conundrum," and there's nothing Pen, Jasper, and I like better than to argue about a conundrum. We can go on for days.

The only solution for Mrs. Grauche was bangs, but her hair was scraped back away from her face into a bun that hunched on top of her head like a grumpy toad. Maybe she didn't think the eyebrow thing was a big deal. Maybe she was too busy tormenting orphans to concern herself with facial hair.

We turned to Denny, who was watching us, waiting for our reaction.

"Why didn't she—" I began in a whisper.

"Bangs weren't in style then," said Denny with a shrug.

"That's a shame," said Jasper.

"So there you have them," Denny said. "You three showed a lot of willpower not laughing out loud. We orphans used to dare each other to come in here and not laugh. I never lasted more than a minute."

"I don't blame you," said Jasper. "Aren't portraits supposed to show you at your best?"

"Oh, they *do* show them at their best," said Denny. "In person they were both, in their own way, much more . . ."

"Disagreeable?" I supplied automatically. "Unpleasant? Morally repugnant?"

Denny laughed. "You've got an impressive vocabulary for a kid who doesn't say much. What did you do—memorize the thesaurus?"

"Certain parts of it, yeah," I admitted.

As I said this, the temperature in the room seemed to drop from summer to winter in the space of five words. The three living boys noticed immediately.

Jasper shivered. "What's happening?" he said.

"What do you mean?" Denny asked.

"It's suddenly freezing in here," I said.

"Um," said Pen. "I hate to interrupt the weather report, but . . ."

"But what?" Denny asked. "What's gotten into you thr—"

But then he saw it. We all did.

Pen was pointing at the desk on the right. Where a brass paperweight in the shape of a bulldog (maybe? or a pug?) was inching its way across the dusty blotter. Toward us.

"I think that's our cue to skedaddle," Denny whispered.

But before we could, the bulldog (pug?) launched from the desk and flew directly at us.

16

THE FOUR OF US DROPPED TO the floor as if the rug had been pulled out from under our feet. Even Denny, who had no substance, ducked, out of some post-death survival instinct. The brass dog whizzed above us, hitting the portrait of Pritchard Grauche smack in the nose and leaving a gash in the canvas.

We didn't bother to stand up again. We did that Marine-training-style crawling thing out of that room so fast, I bet real Marines would have been impressed. Especially since none of us had ever done it before.

We slumped in the hallway for a moment to catch our breath. Except Denny, obviously.

"Was that meant for us?" I asked. "Or the painting?"

"Maybe both," said Jasper. "Maybe the poltergeist was hoping it would bounce off each of our heads and then hit both paintings, like a skipping stone."

"Not *my* head," said Denny, passing his hand through it just to show off.

"Awesome," said Pen.

"I've been remembering some things," Franny announced when we made it back to the porch. "Now that I've had time to think."

"About what?" asked Denny.

"About SPEC," she said. "I worked in the office when I was old enough to open the mail and do the filing. The Gs spent a lot of time cozying up to rich philanthropists to get them to donate money. They went on and on about how they were a childless couple and loved children and wanted to help them and blah blah blah. Nothing could have been further from the truth. They spent almost all the money they were given on themselves. But they did *give* money to one organization—and that was SPEC. I'm pretty sure that the ship they went down on—the *Gigantic*—was chartered by SPEC to go to a SPEC conference in England."

"That would explain the weird lecture they were giving when it sank," said Jasper.

"And the fiery fate of the bunny books," Pen added.

"I remember seeing newsletters from SPEC," said

Franny. "You know that crummy old saying about how children should be seen and not heard? SPEC's slogan was 'Children should be neither seen nor heard.' The articles in the newsletters were about things like 'Keep Children Out of Our Public Parks' and 'What Are Children Doing Cluttering Up Our Schools?'"

"So the Gs got money from people who wanted to help kids, then turned around and gave it to people who hated kids," Jasper said.

"After they were done stocking up on tacky knick-knacks," I said.

"That about sums it up," said Franny.

"So why hasn't anyone from SPEC been here lately?" Pen asked.

"A crackpot organization like that probably just died out after a while," said Charlie.

"Especially if none of them had kids," Denny added.

"So who does the house belong to now?"

"Us, it looks like," said Denny. "Lucky, lucky us."

"I'm not sure you can own a place that's keeping you prisoner," said Theo.

"No," said Charlie. "More like it owns us."

Ghosts are kind of mournful to begin with, but gloomy ghosts are really depressing.

Jasper looked at his watch and said, "We need to go. My mom made me promise to be home for lunch."

Pen and I nodded.

We were standing up, getting ready to leave, saying our goodbyes, when a new ghost appeared on the porch steps. Each time it happened, it was a little less of a shock. This one was a girl who looked about Franny's age, with a long ponytail and a chirpy voice. "Hi," she said to us. "I'm Lorna. I'm on perimeter patrol today. Nice to meet you three! Where are you from, anyway?"

"Nice to meet you, too!" said Pen. "We're from right here in Frog Lake, and we—"

"How about we go over our biographical details later," said Denny. "Lorna? Do you have something to report?"

"Right," said Lorna with a little salute. "Stick to business. Got it. I came here to report that I saw a kid headed our way. Through the woods."

"A kid? Coming here?" said Theo. "What for?"

"I don't know," said Lorna. She studied the three of us for a moment. "He's older than these boys," she said. She studied me in particular. "Do you have an older brother?" she asked. "Because he looks exactly like—"

"Quasimodo?"

"Uh," said Lorna, "I meant he looks a lot like—"

"Was he wearing a purple Lord Lawnchair T-shirt?" I asked.

"Yes, he was."

"Uh-oh," I said. "Neil."

How was it that he managed to be all up in my business when he wasn't wanted and nowhere to be found when he was?

"Neil is Aldo's brother," Pen told the ghosts. "He's our archnemesis."

"We can't let him find us here," said Jasper.

"No kidding," I said. "I wouldn't be allowed beyond the backyard for the rest of the summer if he told my parents we were here."

"I wouldn't be allowed out of my room," said Pen. "And my room is really small."

"Overprotective parents," said Franny longingly.

"Hard to imagine, isn't it?" Theo said.

"We have to stop him from even finding this place," I said. "If Neil found an abandoned orphanage, he probably *would* set it on fire. After bringing his loser friends in to trash it first."

Theo's eyes lit up. "Should we let him?" he asked.

Franny shook her head. "I don't think burning the house down would help after all," she said. "What Jasper said about that made sense, unfortunately. We'd be trapped in the smoking rubble instead."

"Then let's get rid of him," said Denny.

"How?" Lorna asked.

Denny barked out a laugh. "We're ghosts," he said. "We'll do it the old-fashioned way."

"FIRST," SAID DENNY, "YOU THREE HAVE to get back through the woods to the field before your brother does. He has to think you've been there the whole time."

"But we weren't there the whole time," Pen objected. "He saw us not being there."

"Believe me," said Denny, "when I get done with him, he won't know what he saw or didn't see. Go to the field and make like you've been there all morning. And when he gets there, tell him he looks pale and confused. Act concerned about his health."

"I don't know if I *can* act concerned about Neil," I said.

Denny ignored this. "Insist on walking him home. Tell him you think he's had too much sun."

I wished now that I'd taken drama camp more seriously. The role of concerned brother was *not* going to be easy. Fourth fork from the left wasn't even a speaking part.

"On it," said Pen excitedly. "Should I go for a simple 'worried friend of a younger brother' or more like 'fascinated and informed future doctor'?"

"Whatever you want," said Denny.

"I'm thinking future doctor," said Pen. "More believable."

"I'll lure him away from the hedge first," said Denny. "When I whistle, you run for it. Don't stop until you reach the field. Got it?"

We nodded.

"Oh, and guys?" Denny added. "Take those helmets and pads off. Try to tone down the dork, okay? We don't want your archnemesis asking awkward questions."

He glided quickly over to the hedge and passed through it without slowing down.

"Awesome," said Pen.

Denny might have been kind of obnoxious, but he did have moves.

We stowed our protective gear in our backpacks, said goodbye to the other ghosts, and ran over to the tunnel.

We crouched, waiting for Denny's whistle. We were tense, we're willing to admit that. Plus, we were crouching, which isn't a comfortable waiting position. So we may have jumped the gun when we heard the whistle.

A whistle, anyway. Denny's whistle? A bird's whistle? We didn't stop to think. We heard a whistle and we scooted through the hedge. When we were clear, we scrambled to our feet and started to run.

It's hard to run through woods, as we'd already found out. You have to watch where you're going if you don't want to lose an eye, which would make it even harder to watch where you're going. So we were mostly running but also partly bumbling through the woods.

I was in the lead, maybe because I'm a faster runner than Pen or Jasper. Or maybe, as both Pen and Jasper want to point out, because I was the most eager to get away from Neil. Anyway, Pen and Jasper were behind me, they want me to be sure to mention, when all three of us ran straight into my horrific brother.

Neil isn't a big kid, but he's taller than any of us and solid. Like a side of beef, only less attractive. If it had been just me crashing into him, he wouldn't have fallen. If it had been me and Pen or Jasper, he probably wouldn't have fallen. But the three of us took him down. Hard.

He flailed around on the ground for a moment, which was kind of fun to see even though the three of us were flailing around down there too. He started swearing as soon as he stood up and realized what it was—*who* it was—that had knocked him over.

We can't quote what he said because this is a school project. We'll reduce it down for the sake of politeness. Imagine that Neil's speech is spaghetti sauce and his swears are big chunks of onion, and since you don't like onion, you have pulled the chunks out and lined them up along the rim of your plate. This is what was left:

"You . . . dipsticks. You complete and total . . . What the . . . are you doing running around like . . . out here. You almost broke my . . . ing . . . , you little . . ."

It turns out there's not much left to this sauce when you take out the onions. So never mind. If you have an older brother and ever knocked him down so hard that he had to kind of roll around and then stumble when he tried to stand up and then rub dirt off his brand-new concert T-shirt that he paid for with his own money, you can fill in the blanks.

As Neil was finishing up the first round of shouting at us and taking a breath for the next one, Denny appeared behind him. Denny made the international "keep quiet" motion with his forefinger over his mouth and then the international "back off" motion with two hands.

We backed off, which didn't surprise Neil; most people back off when he's yelling at them—or even just talking to them. Then Denny glided around between us and Neil so Neil could see him.

Neil had finished taking a breath, but instead of more shouting at us, he had to use it on Denny. "Who are you?" he asked—rudely, we might add. He looked Denny up and down. Also rudely. "And what the . . . [onion chunk] are you wearing?"

Did I mention that Neil's personality could use some tweaking? Especially in terms of first impressions?

"You don't know me," said Denny in a low, quiet voice we hadn't heard him use before. "And you don't want to know me."

"Got that right," Neil muttered. "So why don't you beat it, okay, kid? We're kind of in the middle of something here."

"I'm not going anywhere," said Denny. "But you are. You are going to leave these woods and never come back."

"Or what?" said Neil. He said it in his usual tone, but he took a step away from Denny as he said it, and he had a twitchy look on his loathsome face that I recognized as nervousness. It's not that Denny was anywhere near Neil's size or looked like he could kick Neil's butt, but he was a ghost, and there was definitely something eerie about him.

"Or I'm going to do some things you're not going to like," said Denny. And he moved closer to Neil without taking a step.

We're pretty sure Neil noticed this, so what he did next

was impressive—we'll give him that. He stayed put and he shrugged. Then he said, "Seems like there are four of us and one of you."

Which was hilarious for a couple reasons. First, that Neil would include three non-tough-looking middle schoolers in his fighting lineup. And second, that he assumed we would take his side after what he'd been yelling at us moments ago.

"I don't know what you're talking about," said Denny. "There's only you and me out here."

"What are you, bonkers?" said Neil. "My brother and his friends are standing right behind you."

Denny laughed. Not his usual laughing-at-our-expense laugh. This was, apparently, his creepy-ghost laugh. And it was effective.

"There's no one behind me," said Denny. And before any of us could think of getting out of the way, he backed right through us. Not all three of us, obviously. He wasn't three people wide. He backed through half of Jasper and half of me. It felt as if a freezing-cold mist had blown through us. It was hard not to shudder. But Denny wasn't done. He passed through us (half of me and half of Pen this time) again the other way and got right up in Neil's face on the return.

"Uh," said Neil. And he took another step away from Denny.

"Just you and me out here in the woods," said Denny in a soft but menacing way. It seemed like he was rising up on tiptoe, but he was actually rising off the ground to the point that Neil had to look up at him instead of down. "And I'd rather you weren't here. Got it?" He reached out a finger to jab Neil's chest for emphasis. The finger went into Neil's chest and stayed there.

Neil yelped.

"Got it?" Denny repeated.

Neil was looking down at his chest, which appeared to have this kid's finger buried in it up to the second knuckle and must have felt as if an icicle were lodged in there. He didn't say anything.

Denny's head swiveled 180 degrees toward us, and he whispered, "Run. Now."

We did.

18

WE WERE SITTING ON THE SOCCER field, still panting from our run but not too badly, when Neil staggered out of the woods.

He was pale and sweating and he looked like he'd seen a ghost—sorry, but there's no other way to put it. The three of us stood up, and we put on our fake worried faces. Which wasn't hard. He was that pathetic.

"Neil," I said as he got near us. "Are you okay? You look awful." No acting required there.

He bent over and put his hands on his knees, waiting to catch his breath. When he did, he said, "What happened to you guys? Where did you go?"

The three of us exchanged glances of confusion and

increasing concern. Pen's was really good, Jasper and I will readily admit.

"What do you mean, where did we go? We've been here all morning. Where have *you* been?" I asked.

"What? I just met you in the woods. Before that . . . that kid showed up."

"We weren't in the woods," I said. "I don't know who you saw, but it wasn't us."

"How did you get into the woods?" Jasper asked Neil. "We never saw you come past here." The three of us, comparing notes later, admitted that we were all dying to high-five each other at the brilliance of this.

"I came right by here, like, half an hour ago," said Neil. "I was looking for Aldo." He was definitely not in his right mind if he was calling me Aldo and not Typo. "Mom wanted me to tell you to come home," he said to me. "You weren't here."

"Yes we were," I said. "We were sitting right here half an hour ago."

"Neil, you seem confused," said Pen in a calm future-doctor voice. His early training as a candelabra was definitely paying off. "And you're very sweaty. Looks like severe hydrochondria to me. I think you've been out in the sun too long."

(Do we need to tell you that there's no such word or condition as "hydrochondria"? Probably not.)

"What happened to your Lord Lawnchair shirt?" I couldn't help but add, just to rub it in. "It's all dirty. It's brand-new, isn't it?"

Neil sank down onto the grass. "The weirdest thing happened to me," he said. "Some kid in the woods . . ."

"Beat you up?" I asked.

"What? No!" said Neil, and Jasper gave me a look that meant *Don't push it.* "No one beat me up. It was . . . strange, is all. He— Never mind. I need a drink. Do you have any water?"

I handed him my water bottle, and he chugged half of it down. He tried to return it, but it was full of his backwash, so I told him to keep it.

"You need to continue hydrating," Jasper told him. "And get into the shade. That's what you do when you've had too much sun."

"Let's get you home," said Pen, still the concerned future professional.

Neil heaved a big sigh and stood up. He poured the rest of the water over his head. "Yeah," he said. "That's probably a good idea."

So we took Neil home, as instructed, continuing to deny that we'd been in the woods at all. He got less and less sure of himself the more lies we piled on. Meanwhile, we got more and more sure of ourselves each time we repeated our story. I kept asking him what had happened with the kid in the woods, but he refused to say anything more about it.

Mom took one look at him when we got inside and said, "Neil, are you okay?"

"We think he might have had too much sun," said Pen. "He's all pale and sweaty and confused."

"I gave him my water," I said.

Mom made Neil go lie down with a bottle of sports drink and a cool washcloth for his forehead.

"I sent him to find you almost an hour ago," she said when she got back to the kitchen. "Do you know what happened to him?"

"We were at the soccer field all morning," I said. "And then a few minutes ago he wandered out of the woods."

She shook her head. "I was going to take you to the lake for lunch," she said. "But Neil's not going anywhere like that. Sorry."

Jasper, Pen, and I ate the picnic lunch my mom had made to take to the lake. It was good—no test recipes—but it would have been better at the lake. Which somehow made me annoyed with Neil, though even I knew that wasn't fair.

Later, the three of us were sitting on the floor of my room, the ghost book in front of us. We were arguing about the technical differences between poltergeists and other types of ghosts, which is why we didn't hear my disgusting brother sneak up on us.

"What's that?" he asked, peering at the book, which Pen immediately slammed shut. That didn't help, because the cover then screamed *The Big Book of Hauntings: A Comprehensive Guide to Ghosts and Other Specters* at Neil.

"Why are you three reading about ghosts?" he asked, not in a chitchatting way.

"It's for school," Jasper said. "A summer reading assignment."

Neil grabbed the book and flipped it over. "No, it's not," he said, reading the description on the back. "No way is something this interesting an assignment for school."

He had us there.

He stopped reading the book cover and started reading us. Carefully. "You *were* out there in the woods today, weren't you," he said. And no, there shouldn't be a question mark at the end of that sentence. It wasn't a question. "And you saw that kid, didn't you." Again, not a question, certainly not one we were going to answer.

"No, we didn't see any kid, because we weren't there and there was no kid," Pen blurted. "Maybe it was a hologram. Did you think of that?"

Pen admits now that this wasn't his finest moment in the story so far.

"Maybe *what* was a hologram?" said Neil. This *was* a question, but none of us responded.

In fact, Jasper calmly went back to our cover story with: "Should you be out of bed? You still look kind of pale."

We're sure our faces did look concerned at this point, just not for Neil. More because of him.

"Shut it, Yi," said Neil. "I'm not buying any of that garbage. You saw something in those woods too. And then you tried to convince me I was hallucinating. Why would you do that, huh, Typo? What twerpy reason would you three have for doing that?"

Nate the Great he wasn't, but he was getting too close for comfort.

"Mom!" I yelled. "Neil's still acting weird and he's bothering us!"

Neil walked out of my room, turned, and stood in the doorframe. We knew he was trying to look menacing, but that didn't mean he didn't. He pointed two fingers at his eyes and then at us. "I'm watching you three insects," he said.

He turned and walked down the hall as my mom came up the stairs.

19

WE DIDN'T GET TO GO BACK to the orphanage for three days. The day after the whole Neil incident, we had to lie low because we knew he would follow us wherever we went. In fact, we deliberately did the most boring things we could think of, just to mess with him.

It was Jasper's idea to go stand in front of the barbershop and watch guys get their hair cut. Eventually, Mike, the owner, came out and asked us to go away—we were giving his customers the creeps.

The next day it poured, so we were glad to stay inside. My toad-faced brother doesn't have a long attention span, so by the morning of the third day, we figured it was safe to go if we left before Neil woke up. As an added precaution, we took a roundabout route.

When we got to the front steps of the orphanage, we waited for the usual ghosts to show up, which they eventually did. Except for Stella, who was shy and also probably afraid of mean Jasper, and Charlie and Lorna, who were working double patrol around the hedge.

"Did you ditch the nosy brother?" Denny asked.

"Yep," said Pen.

"Did I put a good fright into him?" Denny asked. "I tried to go easy on him, but he's a stubborn customer, isn't he? Had to turn up the dial a few notches." He nodded happily. "I've never haunted someone before. It's a hoot. You should try it, Franny."

"I think not," she said primly.

"I'll go with you next time," said Theo. "I've been practicing my moaning, and I think it's getting good."

"Can I hear it?" said Pen. "I've never heard an authentic ghost moan before."

"Sure, when I've got it perfected," said Theo.

"Do you want to hear my future-doctor impression?" Pen asked him.

"You definitely freaked Neil out," Jasper told Denny as Pen asked Theo what had brought him to the doctor today. "We had him convinced he had heatstroke. For a while, anyway."

"What do you mean, a while?"

"He saw us reading the ghost book later and got suspicious," I admitted.

"Do you think he'll come back?"

"Not here. He doesn't know this place exists," I said. "He might go back to the woods, though. He knows something's up, and he definitely has nothing better to do."

Neil was like a wad of chewed gum: glued to the bottom of your shoe on a hot day, but nowhere in sight when you needed to stick it on the end of a pole to get something out of a storm drain.

"Maybe we should cover up the tunnel through the hedge," said Franny.

"Then how would we get through?" asked Pen.

"You boys can make a new one on the far side after you fill in the old one," said Franny.

None of us had a bossy older sister, but we were getting an idea of what it might be like.

"There are some gardening tools in the shed out back," said Denny a bit too eagerly.

"Those ghosts are lucky they have no substance," muttered Pen as his heavy, man-size shovel hit yet another rock. We were digging up a stubborn section of hedge on the far side—where the fence was missing enough rails—planning to fill in the hole on the side closest to the soccer field. "It means we get stuck with all the dirty work."

"And why won't Neil find the new tunnel?" Jasper asked. "This seems like a waste of time." He wasn't digging, due to his wrist, only making what he (and he alone) thought were helpful suggestions.

"This side of the hedge doesn't connect to the woods by the field," I said. I'd managed to peer through the new hole and have a look. "I think the woods here go down to the stream behind the library."

"That's good," said Pen. "When we cross the stream, the water will erase our scent."

"Our *scent*?" Jasper repeated. "Neil isn't a bloodhound. He's not going to be following us by smell. Although probably anyone could follow you two by your smell now."

"Digging is sweaty work," I said, "as you would know if you were contributing anything besides—"

"Maybe that brother of yours will just follow the sound of your complaining," said Denny, appearing a few feet away from and above us.

"Ack! Don't sneak up on us when we're shoveling," said Pen, who had been startled into throwing a spadeful of dirt in my face.

"If you quit your bellyaching, it'll go quicker," said Denny. He lay back in the air as if he were lounging by a pool. He even crossed his ankles. "You kids need to build up some calluses on those soft little hands of yours. Anyway, I've been sent to tell you to come back to the porch when you're finished. We've got things to go over. So step it up."

"What kind of things?" asked Pen.

But Denny had disappeared.

We kept our complaints to a minimum after that. Not because we were afraid Neil was lurking around, but because we figured Denny might be.

When we had the old tunnel filled and looking as natural as possible and the new one big enough to crawl through and also camouflaged with some extra branches (my idea, thank you), we staggered back to the porch and collapsed.

"We've taken inventory," said Franny, appearing as we chugged most of the water in our water bottles and I used the rest of mine to rinse my dirt-spattered face. "Or maybe roll call."

"Huh?" Jasper said, squinting up at her. The sun was behind her, and she looked solid, but she didn't cast a shadow. Yes, weird. "What kind of roll call?"

"We did some brainstorming over the past few days," said Franny. "We decided that whatever the thing is that's got us trapped here—"

"The poltergeist," Pen supplied.

"Right. We decided it's probably a former resident. Why hang around here if you don't have a connection to the place? Why not spend your death someplace nice if you can?"

"Like on your boat," said Theo wistfully.

"And we figured it isn't either of the Gs," Franny continued. "Or even both of them together. After all, hearing their own names wouldn't bother them. It has to be someone who (A) lived here, and (B) hated them. Which means an orphan. Follow?"

We nodded, though there were some gaps in this logic that any of us could have pointed out (and did point out among ourselves later). Just putting in (A) and (B) points doesn't make your argument logical. As the three of us knew all too well, having barely gotten through the outlining unit in Mr. Mullins's class last year.

"So, by process of elimination, whoever isn't here as a ghost is likely the poltergeist. Right?" said Franny.

More not-quite-convinced nodding.

"It was fairly easy to figure out who isn't here," said Charlie. "We went down the alphabet: Bump, Clump, et cetera, all the way to Wally Wump. And everyone's accounted for except one orphan."

Franny was nodding, eager to jump back in. "An interesting one, actually." She shrugged. "Maybe she's being shy. She was quite a bit younger than the rest of us. But no one has been able to find her."

"What was her name?" Jasper asked.

"Greta," said Franny.

A strange thing happened when Franny said the name. I was the only one who saw it. Franny was looking at us, and everyone else was looking at Franny. Except me. I had turned toward the house because I heard a noise coming from inside. A small noise, like a sighing sound. And then, when Franny had finished saying "Greta," I saw it.

The window nearest to us fogged up, like someone had breathed on it. By the time I had said, "Hey, look at the window . . . ," the fog had disappeared.

20

NO ONE BELIEVED ME ABOUT THE fog. They said some dirt must have gotten in my eyes while we were shoveling and fogged my vision. Why, you might ask, would *actual ghosts* not believe that someone had seen a supernatural-type thing? Search me. Maybe even ghosts only believe what they can see with their own ghost eyes.

So I was the only one who watched the window as Franny told the story of Greta Grump, and the other ghosts chimed in from time to time to fill in the gaps.

Greta, they said, was the one baby who ever came to the orphanage. Most orphaned babies, they said, got adopted right away and never ended up at a crummy orphanage like the Grauches'.

Mrs. G brought Greta to the orphanage herself. She had been away at a fancy health spa, "tending to her nerves," Franny said. "She was always complaining that we kids made her nervous and fluttering her handkerchiefs and claiming she needed smelling salts. Like a ninny."

Mrs. G said a woman she'd met at the spa had given Greta to her. Greta, the woman told Mrs. G, was the daughter of a neighbor who'd run off with a carnival. Or maybe been run over by a carnival. Franny couldn't remember the details, and none of the other ghosts had heard anything about where Greta came from.

"We didn't care," Theo admitted. "Most of us were a lot older than she was. Not interested in a baby."

Franny nodded. "I'm sorry to say she was simply more work for the rest of us, someone else to take care of and clean up after. She was a toddler when the Gs went down with the *Gigantic*. She went to a foster family when the orphanage closed, like the rest of us."

"Except me," said Charlie. "I went back to my real family."

"That's right, Charlie, keep rubbing it in," said Denny.

"It's just a fact," said Charlie.

He and Denny eyed each other for a long, uncomfortable moment.

"So maybe Greta isn't here because she wasn't part of the group," Jasper suggested—reasonably, we thought.

Franny shook her head. "Neither were a few others who were younger, but we've spoken to them."

"Also," said Denny, turning his back on Charlie, "we all look about the age we were when Greta was here—right before the place closed."

"But if the poltergeist is Greta," Jasper pressed, "the question is why. Why would she haunt a place she could barely remember? I mean, I don't remember much from when I was a toddler."

"Do you remember attacking me with a plastic shovel?" Pen asked him.

"That was preschool," said Jasper. "And no."

"I have a shovel-shaped scar, thanks to you!"

"You got that scar bowling," said Jasper.

There was a silence as we seemed to hit a dead end.

Which gave me an opening to go back to the topic of the window. I'd been keeping an eye on it as Franny and the other ghosts talked about Greta. An eye whose vision was perfectly clear.

As we talked about Greta, the window had fogged up again several times—each time Greta's name was mentioned, it seemed to me. Then the fog would disappear. The window was dirty, so the other thing I noticed I'm less sure of. But I'm still almost certain it happened. The window fogged up as Franny was talking about Mrs. G bringing Greta back from the spa. And then, before the fog went away, I saw a handprint appear in it. It looked exactly as if someone had pressed a hand to the glass. But there was no hand—only the print. Which was gone seconds later.

No orphan ghost could have done that, since, as we've already established, their hand would have passed through the glass of the window.

I told the others what I'd seen, but it wasn't until I mentioned that what I'd seen helped their case that they decided maybe I didn't have dirt in my eyes.

"Look," I said, "if the poltergeist is Greta, maybe she's attracted to the sound of her name, the same way she seems to hate the Gs' names. So she came to the window when we started talking about her, and she reacted each time her name was mentioned. Makes sense, right?"

"I suppose it does," said Franny. She wasn't exactly jumping up and down and saying "Aldo, you genius!" but I'm sure that's what she meant.

Pen and Jasper are equally sure that's not what she meant, but whatever. We'll agree to disagree. We're good at that.

"If Aldo is right," said Denny, "there are two things to consider. The first is that the poltergeist—Greta, let's assume for now—can hear and respond to what we say."

"We sort of knew that already from the way she acts when anyone says the Gs' full names," said Jasper.

"Or SPEC's," said Pen.

"Or describes the Gs' portraits," I said.

"Okay, then this is more evidence of that," said Denny. "But even more important, I think, is that she—if it is she—doesn't always respond violently."

"True," said Franny. "If she did press her hand to the window while we were talking about her, that seems sort of . . . forlorn, really."

There was a sniffle from a cobweb near the porch roof.

"Stella," Franny whispered to us. "She's very softhearted."

"The point being," said Denny, "that it's possible our poltergeist can be reasoned with."

"Sherlock Dump, on the case," said Charlie sarcastically.

"What is with you today?" Denny asked him.

"What's with *you*?" was Charlie's response.

"Chump," Denny muttered.

"Boys!" said Franny. "Settle down and act your age. Your *real* age," she clarified. "Aldo," she said to me, "how big was the handprint you saw on the window?"

"How big?"

"Yes. Would you say the hand that made it was bigger or smaller than yours?"

I thought about it. Then I went over to the window and put my hand against it for comparison. "Smaller. Definitely smaller than mine."

"There you have it," said Franny. "If Greta's experience is anything like ours, she's part who she was when she lived here, no matter how old she was when she died. She's part small child. And sometimes young children fly off the handle. Sometimes much older ones do too," she added with a stern look at Denny and Charlie.

"So Greta can be reasoned with, but only like you'd reason with a little kid?" I asked. I shook my head, picturing Pen's seven-year-old twin sisters. "That's not going to be easy."

Jasper and Pen, picturing the same thing, nodded grimly.

21

OUR ASSIGNMENT FOR THAT AFTERNOON WAS to come up with ways to talk to the poltergeist, who we'll call Greta, because we were assuming that's who it was. Talking to her wasn't really the problem, we agreed. Talking to her without being clocked with actual clocks was.

We left through the new tunnel in the hedge and ended up walking along the stream behind the library until we came to the library itself. We decided to stop in and do some more research.

We split up again. Pen, whose case of the heebie-jeebies around the local-history room's librarian was no better, went back to the nonfiction stacks to do some in-depth reading about communicating with poltergeists.

Jasper and I went back to the local-history room to see if we could find out anything about Greta Grump.

The library's air-conditioning wasn't working, and it was hot in there. It was especially hot in the local-history room, which was in the old part of the library. There was a big fan sitting on the librarian's desk, one of those rotating ones that blasts you with air every few seconds and then turns away to let you heat up before it comes back to blast you again.

We didn't know where to start. We tried a few books on the history of the town, but none of their indexes had anyone named Grump. We looked at the town census for her birth record, but we didn't know exactly when she was born, and besides, as Jasper pointed out, she wasn't born here; Mrs. Grauche had brought her from the spa, and before that, no one knew what her story was, except that it maybe involved a carnival. We wondered about marriage records, but we had no idea what year she may or may not have gotten married. We considered death records, but again, no date. We were stumped.

Which left us with one thing to do. We didn't want to do it. In fact, it was something we hated to do. But we had to do it if we wanted to know more. Which we did. And that meant we were going to have to . . .

Pen and Jasper think this whole buildup is a waste of time and not at all suspenseful. I can't help but agree with them. We can rework it later.

Anyway, Jasper and I decided that our only hope was to do something we hated: Ask an Adult for Help.

We went over to stand in front of the librarian's vast desk. She was reading, her head tilted down toward the book, her thick bangs falling across her also-thick-but-in-a-different-way glasses. We shuffled around a little, and Jasper made a polite throat-clearing noise. She looked up. And as she looked up, the fan turned toward her and hit her with a blast of air.

As the air rushed at the librarian's face, it lifted—for a moment—the curtain of her bangs. The never-before-seen (by us) top rims of her glasses were exposed. Along with her forehead. But that's not why we're describing this particular scene in such detail. Who cares if we saw the local-history room librarian's forehead? There's nothing that interesting about foreheads. But it wasn't her forehead that caught our attention. Or the top rims of her glasses. It was the area between those things.

Pen and Jasper think that, again, my attempt at suspenseful buildup is flopping hard. Unless a gooey alien is about to spring from the librarian's skull, they say, it is pointless to go on and on like this. But I disagree. It may not be an alien—there are no aliens in this journal, FYI—but what we are about to see is really important. A major turning point, even if it is just something we noticed about a lady's head.

Because between the librarian's glasses and forehead, almost always hidden under her bangs, was a clue. Not *a* clue, really, but three clues. The local-history room librarian, we discovered in that fateful moment, had three eyebrows.

22

"MAY I HELP YOU, BOYS?" THE librarian asked as her bangs fluttered back down into place.

"Um, ah," I managed to say.

"We need . . . We were looking for . . . ," Jasper eked out.

We're guessing the librarian frowned (times three) at this point, but we don't know for sure because her forehead wasn't visible anymore.

"Speak up," she said. And now she was tapping one fingernail on the desk, which never helps anyone gather their thoughts.

One of us was about to speak up. Both of us now say that he was the one who was about to speak up. But at that crucial point we saw, in the doorway to the local-history room, the last thing we wanted or expected to see at the library today or any other day.

Neil.

He saw us seeing him and waved in a fake-friendly way.

None of us waved back.

The librarian's fingernail paused midtap, hovering above the desk.

Jasper and I knew we couldn't ask the librarian anything about Greta Grump with Neil eavesdropping.

"Uh, actually, we're good," Jasper said to her quickly. "All good. Sorry to have bothered you. We'll show ourselves out."

I'm not sure what he meant by that last thing or why he said it with a British accent. Neither is he.

Neil had slithered off by the time Jasper and I saw ourselves out of the local-history room. We went to find Pen in the nonfiction stacks.

He was sitting on the floor, blocking an aisle, with several books in front of him.

"I hit the jackpot," he said. "There are whole books on poltergeists, if you can believe it. Check these out."

We did check them out (library humor there, which Jasper doesn't appreciate, but too bad). And when we got outside, Jasper and I told Pen what we'd seen in the local-history room.

He was unimpressed.

"So she has three eyebrows," he said. "So what? Maybe lots of people have three eyebrows and we're more aware of them now. You know, like if you get a new pair of sneakers and suddenly it seems like everyone has the same kind?"

"Can you think of any other people you've ever met in your entire life with three eyebrows?" Jasper asked him. He (Jasper) shook his head. "It has to mean something."

"But what?" I said. "The only thing it *seems* to mean is that the librarian is related to Ermaline Grauche. Who didn't have any children. Because she hated them."

"Maybe she had a three-eyebrowed sister who had kids, and the librarian is her niece or something," said Pen.

"There's no such word as 'eyebrowed,'" said Jasper.

"There is now," said Pen. "Three-eyebrowed. Tri-browed. Tribrows, get it? She has tribrows instead of eyebrows."

No one laughed (including you, probably). I didn't think it was that funny, Pen at least had the dignity not to laugh at his own joke, and Jasper wasn't listening. He was noticing something behind us. Something hideous of form and feature.

"Neil is still following us," he whispered.

We couldn't even ditch him in nonfiction.

This was getting serious.

23

IT WAS PAST LUNCHTIME WHEN I got home. Neil had beat me there and was lounging on the sofa, looking smug.

Mom was in the kitchen, struggling to chop up a giant vegetable that looked like something she'd found by the side of the road. In a smoking crater. Glowing. I sincerely hoped that no part of it would ever appear on a plate anywhere near me.

"Aldo," she said when she got a good eyeball full of me, "why are you so filthy? What have you been doing now?"

"Nothing."

"Then why is your face dirty? And your shirt? You look like you've been digging a ditch."

"I don't know."

She put down her giant cleaver and gave me a look she has. It is a look that tells you she's not buying your floundering efforts to put her off and you'd better come up with something convincing *now*. So I did.

"Jasper and Pen and I *were* digging," I said, working off her cue. Then, out of the corner of my eye, I saw Neil's antennae go up. Not literally. He doesn't actually have antennae. That I know of.

He was suddenly engrossed in one of our dad's gardening-supplies catalogs, pretending not to be listening. Which told me that he was listening. So I added, in a jovial, can-you-believe-the-wacky-things-we-kids-get-up-to voice, "We were digging for treasure. In the woods. Just for fun."

And with that, the disgusting poop-eating fly was snared in the clever spider's sticky web.

I'm not even going to tell you what Jasper and Pen had to say about that metaphor when they read it. I had to give them each five bucks to leave it in.

Neil disappeared about half an hour later. And this time *I* was the one following *him*. Sure enough, he sneaked out to the shed and got a shovel, then headed for the woods by the soccer field.

I went to Jasper's house, and we called Pen. He brought the poltergeist books, and we started reading, looking for ways to communicate with Greta Grump.

"It says here," said Pen after a while, "that this polter-geist in New Orleans used to write messages for the people who lived in the house."

"How?" Jasper asked.

"I guess the people weren't very good housekeepers, because the poltergeist wrote things in the dust on the furniture."

"Like what?"

Pen read for a while and then said, "Mostly things like 'Get out' and 'Go away.'"

"Nice."

"Yeah. It seemed to want to be alone."

We read on.

"Ha!" said Jasper after a while. His book had goofy-looking cartoon ghosts on the cover, so we didn't have high hopes about the quality of its information. "Here's a poltergeist that kept clogging up the toilets in this mansion."

"Does the orphanage even have toilets?" I asked.

"It must," said Pen. "Mustn't it? Shoot. Now I'm going to worry about having to use the bathroom every time we go there."

"You could use the woods."

Mention of the woods made me think of Neil. I told Pen and Jasper that I'd led him to believe we were digging for treasure in the woods and that he had gone there this afternoon with a shovel.

"He actually fell for it?" Jasper said.

"He's really not very smart, is he?" Pen added.

"I keep telling you that."

"I'd think one of you was adopted, except that you look exactly—"

"He skipped away from the house with a shovel like one of Snow White's roommates on his way to the mine," I said. "I think he was whistling."

According to our books, certain poltergeists got their messages across by writing on walls with icky substances including blood, or by scratching words in glass, et cetera. Why none of them seemed to have a pencil handy wasn't discussed. One poltergeist in Bulgaria drew pictures in the ashes in the fireplace of what it seemed to want to do to the people who lived there. Let's just say these pictures involved bodily harm.

None of the books' poltergeists seemed to be sending pleasant or welcoming messages, but since poltergeists are basically swirling balls of anger, according to the books, that didn't come as a surprise.

So poltergeists could communicate by writing or drawing when they wanted to—that was clear. But if ours was a toddler in poltergeist form, could she do either well enough to let us know what she was so upset about?

There was one way to find out. But first we had to make sure my loathsome brother was too busy to follow us to our new hedge entrance.

It was Pen who came up with an ingenious capper to my already ingenious treasure-digging ruse. He went down the hall to his twin sisters Camden and Acadia's room and came back with a book.

"This is from about three crazes ago—pirates—so they're never going to miss it," he said, handing it to me.

"*X Marks the Spot*," I read off the cover. "*Your Guide to Finding Buried Treasure Near You.* Perfect."

"It's silly, actually," said Pen. "It came with this cheesy metal detector that didn't seem to detect anything but candy wrappers. But Neil might fall for it."

"Oh, he'll fall for it," I said. "I'll make sure he does."

"How?" asked Jasper, who didn't have any siblings.

"Easy," I said. "I'll hide it."

24

I PUT CAM AND CADY'S TREASURE-HUNTING book under some socks in my underwear drawer. And yes, the socks I put on top of it had been pulled out of the dirty laundry. Why not have a little fun with it?

Then I rummaged around in our old art supplies and found some of those huge sheets of paper they give little kids to scribble on and also some of those jumbo crayons they give little kids to scribble with. I put them in my back-pack, which I left in plain sight on the floor of my room, to be sure that Neil wouldn't bother with it.

Speaking of Neil, you should have seen him when he got home, right before dinner. No whistling on his way *back* from the mine, that's for sure. First, to set the scene:

This time I was the one on the sofa, looking smug. I had a tall glass of icy-cold lemonade beside me and a fan sending gentle breezes my way. This positioning wasn't a coincidence. I had seen him coming from my bedroom window.

He staggered into the front hall after dropping the shovel on the front walk (where our dad would later trip over it, leading to a Written Agreement about Careless Tool Usage and Storage). There was so much sweat and dirt on Neil's face, shirt, and arms that mud had formed. His pants were torn. He looked like he'd been wandering in the wilderness for weeks, living off beetles and trying to drink from dried-up streambeds.

I smiled at him. He didn't smile back. I greeted him with a smooth "Hey, bro." (I never call him "bro.") He didn't respond. I sipped my lemonade and settled back onto a cushion. "Nice day for relaxing, isn't it?" I asked.

All in all, a triumph.

I could hear Neil's snoring through his closed bedroom door the next morning. Poor thing was tuckered out from yesterday's digging. I could almost see the Zs floating in the air above him. And the drool on the pillow below him.

I grabbed my pack full of art supplies and went to meet Pen and Jasper outside the library, to take our new route to the orphanage.

A half hour or so later, we were helmeted and padded,

huddling in the doorway to the Grauche Orphanage for Orphans like the world's most losing football team. Our semi-transparent coaches were Franny, Denny, and Theo.

"Stay calm," Franny advised, "and don't do anything to upset her."

"The problem is," Pen said, "that it doesn't seem to take much to upset her, and we don't know what it is until after we've done it."

"Move slowly, speak soothingly, and duck if she starts throwing things," Denny advised. "Also, don't mention SPEC or the Gs and *don't* discuss their portraits. We learned that the hard way, didn't we?"

"Don't worry," said Theo. "We're right behind you."

Pen stepped over the threshold, followed by Jasper, followed by me. I kept turning around to make sure the ghosts were with us, which they were, though Theo was getting blurry.

"Where to?" whispered Pen.

"The office," I said. "So we can spread the paper out on a desk."

Pen tiptoed down the hall, Jasper tiptoed after Pen, I tiptoed after Jasper, and the ghosts glided in a nervous, overlapping mass behind me.

The farther we got inside the house, the drier my throat got and the wetter my armpits got. The reason for this, aside from my general dislike of having objects thrown at my head, was that I had been elected as the spokesperson for this mission. It was not a position I had asked for. Pen and Jasper had outvoted me, based on the fact that I negotiate Written Agreements with my parents all the time and that I had once—and *only* once—successfully negotiated with Cam and Cady.

I had been the one to finally convince them to come out of the bouncy house at their fourth birthday party. And let's be clear about this: It took me two hours of intense negotiating. It was well after dark and all the other party guests had gone to bed by the time I got them to leave. Pen still has to give them piggyback rides whenever they want as part of the deal. He blames me for not putting any age or weight limits on that promise, but I was getting desperate by the time it was over.

We got to the office, and I took off my backpack and set it on a chair. I removed the big sheets of paper and the big crayons and spread them out on one of the desks, as far as I could get them from any heavy desktop tchotchkes. I stepped away from the desk and stood very still.

"Well?" Pen said.

"Go on," said Jasper.

"Soothingly!" added Franny in a non-soothing whisper.

I took a deep breath. I was not only damp all over (except my mouth) by this time, but I was queasy, too. I swallowed hard.

"No puking," said Jasper.

"I'm not going to puke," I lied.

I cleared my throat.

"Ah, Greta?" I said quietly. "Can you hear me? Are you listening?"

Everyone waited for a response. There was none.

Taking this as a goodish sign, I tried again. "Greta? If you're here, we want to talk to you. And we're hoping you'll answer us. We brought some nice paper and crayons for you to write with."

I was using my best kid-wheedling voice, and everyone was nodding approvingly.

"Can you come to the office?" I added.

We waited again.

Nothing. So now I got a little edgy, and my verbal diarrhea may have acted up. "The three of us are looking forward to communicating with you on a personal level, learning more about your history—you know . . . finding out more about the real Greta Grump behind the legend."

I don't know where any of that came from, and I hope never to visit there. Pen and Jasper edged away from me as if this new strain of verbal diarrhea might be contagious.

Then there was a thumping sound from somewhere upstairs.

Pen, Jasper, and I flinched in unison.

"Does that mean she's coming?" I asked no one in particular.

No one answered, mainly because they were busy listening to a new sound. This one was like a bowling ball rolling downstairs one step at a time: *thump, thump-thump, thump.*

When the bowling ball reached the first floor, the thumping stopped.

Then there was a sound of breaking glass. To be more specific, the sound of something hard hitting a sheet of glass, as in: In case of emergency, break glass.

"That sounded like the cabinet in the hall," said Theo.

"What cabinet in the hall?" Jasper asked.

"The one with the old swords in it."

Denny and Franny both yelled the same thing at the same time: "Run!"

25

PEN, JASPER, AND I CHARGED RIGHT through the cloud of ghosts on our way out of the office without even noticing the misty sensation. The idea of swords pushed ghost mist right to the bottom of our noticing list. When we got into the hall, we saw a large case mounted high on the wall past the door to the office. The glass doors had been broken, and the pieces were scattered all over the floor. We would have charged right across the broken glass and out the front door except for one thing. Two things, actually.

Two rusty but still very pointy swords hung in the air between us and the nearest exit. They were scraping each other briskly, like knives being sharpened by a cartoon chef. The scritchy metallic sound made our ears want to dive into our skulls for cover. Then, as if they'd noticed us, the swords stopped scraping and sprang to attention, pointing straight up. Then, to our semi-mesmerized horror, the points moved downward until they were leveled at our hearts.

"Kitchen door!" Denny commanded.

Although we hated to turn our backs on those hovering swords, we headed for the kitchen. We ran down the hallway, the ghosts ahead of us, urging us on. The swords flew close behind us, urging us on in a different and much more effective way. If they had been able to breathe, we would have felt their hot, rusty breath on the backs of our necks. At one point (no sword pun intended), one of them poked my back. I know this because I saw the hole in my T-shirt when I took it off that night.

The poltergeist's trademark shrieking had started as soon as we bolted down the hall, which wasn't helping our concentration. We reached the kitchen with the swords right on our heels, only higher up, and Pen grabbed the knob to the back door and yanked.

"Turn it first," Denny yelled.

Pen fumbled. We really needed to stop leaving him in charge of doors.

"Other way!"

There was a lot of déjà vu as we three tumbled out the

back door and fell over one another and down the back steps for the second time.

The ghosts arrived outside at the same time we did, but more gracefully.

"Shut the door!" Franny cried.

Jasper did, then leaped off the porch without using the steps. Gasping for air, he asked, "Why bother? She can come through it, right?"

"True," said Franny, "but the swords can't."

"Actually," said Theo, "I think they can."

He pointed his chin at the door, which was shuddering in its frame as if it were being whacked by a battering ram. A sword plunged partway through a panel and lodged there, sharp end—needless to say—out.

One of the windowpanes in the door shattered, and the other sword flew through the opening at us. If Theo had been solid flesh, he would have been skewered like a butt-kabob. The sword landed point-down in the tall grass.

"Whoever pulls it out gets to be king," Denny joked half-heartedly.

No one laughed at Denny's attempt to lighten the mood. Instead, we scrambled away from the porch until we were out of sword-throwing range. Then we sank to the grass, and the living among us panted like dogs.

"Well, that was a real eye-opener," said Pen between

pants. "It turns out that this particular Pen is not mightier than the sword after all." He shook his head. "Disappointing."

"Sorry, dude," Jasper said. And then: "Who keeps swords in a building full of kids?"

"Ha," Denny barked. "Mr. G kept them there *because* the building was full of kids. Used to threaten to slice us up if we misbehaved. He once told Roger he'd carve him up like a rump roast."

"Poor Roger," said Franny. She shook her head. Then she looked up. "Theo," she called, "Denny was kidding about getting to be king."

Theo was over by the sword stuck in the ground. He kept trying to grasp at it, but his hands whizzed through it.

"We need to put this back right away," Theo said. "Or Mr. Grauche will be angry."

"Theo?" said Franny. "What are you talking about?"

"If Mr. Grauche finds his sword out here, he'll lock me in the cellar," said Theo, still trying to pull up the sword.

Denny went over to Theo and got between him and the sword. "Theo!" he said. "Look at me! It's Denny. Mr. Grauche isn't here. Are you okay?"

Theo straightened up and shook his head like he had water in his ears. "Whoa," he said. "Where was I just then?"

"You tell us," said Franny.

"I thought I was a kid again," said Theo. "About to be in trouble for leaving this sword out here."

We noticed in the silence following Theo's odd statement that the battering at the back door had stopped.

"If that poltergeist is a toddler, she really needs a nap," said Franny.

"Toddlers can't be reasoned with," I said.

"You must have said something wrong in there," Pen said.

"Me? I was doing my best Cam-and-Cady wheedling," I said.

"Right up until you lost it and went all school counselor on her," said Jasper.

"What could I have possibly said to make her attack us with *actual weapons*? I was nothing but polite and respectful." I glanced around at the group. "Does anyone *else* here think I might have said something wrong? Huh?"

The group sidled away from me uncomfortably.

Just then, Lorna appeared. "Something's happened in the office," she said. "You'd better come and see."

"I am *not* going back in there," Pen said. He spoke for Jasper and me as well. I'd left my backpack, but I didn't care. There were other backpacks in the world.

"You don't need to go in," said Lorna. "You can look in the window. That's how I saw it."

She led us around the side of the orphanage to a set of

tall windows. They were too high up for us to see in, but the ghosts hovered outside them to get a glimpse.

"Interesting," said Denny.

"Isn't it?" Lorna agreed.

"She does have a knack for expressing herself," Franny said.

"Nicely done, if I do say so myself," said Theo.

"What? What?" those of us on the ground yelped, jumping uselessly to try to see what they were seeing.

"There's a stepladder in the shed," said Denny.

"Just tell us!"

"Don't be lazy. It's worth it."

We went to the shed and dragged the stepladder and its clinging spiders over to the office windows. We took turns climbing up and peering in.

"Wow," said Jasper.

"Seriously wow," said Pen.

"The crayons were my idea," I said.

26

DO YOU APPRECIATE HOW WE LEFT you hanging at the end of that chapter, like Lorna and the other ghosts did with us outside the office? If there were a way to make you climb a stepladder to keep reading, we would. (Not really, Pen insists on adding. It's just a figure of speech. We would never make you climb a stepladder. Teachers work hard enough.)

Here's what we saw when we looked in the window.

First, nothing. Because it was light outside and dark inside. We had to cup our hands around our eyes to see anything in there.

Next, the office, exactly as we'd left it. Including my backpack, sitting there taunting me with its nearness.

And finally, the two portraits of the Grauches, which hung on the wall opposite the window. They had been, to put it mildly, defaced. A good word here, because it was their actual faces that had been defaced. With a big preschool-size brown crayon (provided by yours truly).

Have you ever seen a book that a toddler has gotten hold of when they also had hold of a crayon? What about a cranky, nap-deprived toddler who hates the pictures in the book? That's what had happened to the Grauches.

Mr. Grauche had sprouted the classic two giant teeth from his closed mouth. He had a big new handlebar mustache. One eye had been x-ed out, and the other had a fat worm coming out of it. Good stuff. His vast forehead, which provided a nice stretch of clear space, had a big letter *L* on it. Next to the portrait, on the wall, the word continued: "OSER."

"Epic," said Jasper.

Mrs. Grauche had fared no better. The defacer had drawn a time-honored witch wart on her nose and made her nostrils even larger. A mole on her chin had eight legs so it looked like a spider. A thick row of bangs had been added to her forehead, almost but not quite covering the three eyebrows.

"You know who Mrs. G looks like," said Pen, climbing down off the ladder, "now that she has bangs? Besides Miss Viola Swamp, I mean."

The ghosts didn't know, of course. But Jasper and I saw it.

"She looks kind of like the librarian," Jasper said. "In the local-history room. If you add glasses and take away the mean stuff and the bad attitude."

"That's interesting," said Denny patronizingly.

"No, there's more to it than that," said Jasper. "We meant to tell you."

"Tell us what?" Franny asked.

"The librarian in the local-history room," said Jasper, "has three eyebrows. Like Mrs. G. She has bangs, so we only saw the eyebrows after a fan blew her bangs off her forehead."

"Tribrows," put in Pen. "She has tribrows. Get it?"

The ghosts ignored Pen and pondered.

"Coincidence?" said Theo finally.

"Hard to imagine," said Denny.

"Especially if they look alike beyond the eyebrows," said Franny.

"A relative of some kind?" Lorna asked.

"You would think so," said Franny. "Except that Mrs. G didn't have any close relatives. No siblings. No parents. No aunts or uncles or cousins, even. She boasted about not having any relatives 'hanging around her neck, asking for handouts' the way Mr. G's relatives did."

"Strange," said Denny.

"Very," Franny agreed.

We left soon after that with a lot of unexplained weirdness hovering around.

First, Greta's huge tantrum when all I did was politely ask to talk to her. Pen continued to insist that it must have been something I said, and I continued to insist that it wasn't, and Jasper stayed well out of the discussion.

Second, Theo thinking he was a kid again for a moment. Pen figured he'd been freaked out by the sword chase. I figured he'd been freaked out by the sword stabbing his ghost butt cheek. Jasper kept his opinion to himself.

Third, the tribrow thing. Pen maintained that tribrows were more common than we had thought. I countered that the librarian must have been a distant relative of Mrs. G's. Jasper hurried ahead so he wouldn't have to deal with us.

Neil was asleep in a lounge chair on the patio when I got home. But there was a lot of evidence that he'd had a busy day between snoring sessions. His T-shirt was greasy, his face was sooty, and his hair was singed. I followed a trail of wires and springs to the shed, where I found something truly sad. It was a broom handle with two foil pie plates attached to one end. There was a lot of duct tape holding everything together. And next to it on the tool bench, several sheets of paper with complicated instructions for—get this—"making a metal detector with common household objects" that he'd downloaded from the internet. Neil's version didn't look much like the one in the illustration.

Yes, my misguided brother had been in my underwear drawer, rummaging under my dirty socks. He had found the decoy treasure-hunting book and was now attempting to make his own metal detector.

We decided to build on the success of the diversion the next morning while Neil was mowing the lawn. Which he was required to do by his Written Agreement with our parents following his Failure to Find a Summer Job.

We took two shovels from Jasper's shed and went to the woods by the soccer field. We picked a good spot as far away from the old route to the orphanage as possible. And we did some digging. Or Pen and I did some digging, and Jasper-of-the-Sprained-Wrist "kept watch."

Digging is miserable work, as we already knew. There are roots: the small, intertwining ones that are spread all over the place like a net, and the huge, log-size ones that your shovel hits and then bounces off to hit you. There are stones: the small ones that fly into the air as you shovel and pelt you and your fellow shoveler, and the huge ones that your shovel hits, et cetera (see "huge roots" above). There are also bugs. The tiny ones that seem determined to fly into your eyes even though they can't live there, so what's the point? And the big, buzzing ones that annoy you until you go after them with your shovel, which just makes you look deranged.

But sometimes you have to make yourself miserable for a while in order to make your snooping brother even more miserable. After we were done, which we were quickly because it was such nasty work, we made deliberately sloppy attempts to hide our shoveling. We repacked the dirt and even smoothed over most—but not all—of our footprints. Then we left, knowing that Neil and his lower-than-low-tech metal detector would be all over the situation in no time.

When we had watched Neil leave the house carrying a long bag meant for some type of sporting equipment and head for the soccer field, Pen, Jasper, and I went back to the orphanage.

27

THINGS WERE IN A BIT OF a tizzy when we got there.

Pen and Jasper are absolutely forbidding me to use the phrase "a bit of a tizzy" in our journal. They feel it doesn't reflect well on our masculinity or something. I don't get it. They're only words. I have promised Pen and Jasper that I will take the phrase out, so if you just read it, it means I forgot. My bad.

First, as we came up to the porch, we noticed Denny kneeling in the weeds nearby. All I could think about in that moment was that it was a good thing ghosts can't get ticks. Although, as Pen said later, they might get ghost ticks.

"Hey, Denny," said Jasper carefully. "What are you doing?"

"I'm pulling weeds, obviously," said Denny without looking up. "It's my job to keep the front walk clear."

"What front walk?" said Jasper.

Denny stopped what he was doing.

"Will you quit bothering me, you—" he began. Then he seemed to wake up, as if he'd been sleepwalking—or sleepweeding—before. "Sorry," he said, straightening up. "Not sure what got into me there. I used to weed the front walk as a kid." He considered the thick green patch he'd been kneeling in. "Guess the weed ship sailed a long time ago, though." He laughed a little bit, but not in a fun, or even making-fun, way.

Franny and Theo appeared on the porch, wondering where we'd been all morning. We explained about the distraction with Neil, and Denny, at least, approved. But they had something they needed to show us, they said. Inside.

Inside wasn't where we wanted to go. Inside was where bad things happened to us. But they made us.

They led us into the parlor, the one where we'd first met Theo and Franny and Denny. It was still a mess from the attack the first day, but there was more.

Greta had been expressing herself again in crayon. The red one this time. High on the wall, where no living toddler could have reached, she had written in big, messy block letters: "MINE." There wasn't an exclamation point after it, but there didn't need to be. It was clearly a red-crayoned shriek, the kind that toddlers routinely use when something of theirs (or something they think should be theirs) is denied them.

Franny, Theo, and Denny led us down the hallway, where the same word appeared again, much bigger, at waist-level.

And there it was again in the office, on the ceiling.

We tiptoed back outside. (Yes, I did get my backpack, thanks for asking.)

"She's been busy," said Franny.

"No kidding," said Jasper.

Pen shook his head. "You would think, if she considers this place hers, she'd take better care of it. Do you know how much Crayon-B-Gone it's going to take to get all that off?"

"What the heck is Crayon-B-Gone?" Jasper asked.

"Did you ever write on the walls when you were little?"

"No."

"Weirdo."

"Slob."

"Manners," said Franny. Every now and then, you heard the old lady coming out of the girl mouth.

"Crayon-B-Gone is this gunk that gets crayon off walls and wallpaper and stuff," Pen said. "My parents buy it by the case because my little sisters are menaces."

Franny laughed. "I wish they'd had that when my kids were growing up," she said. "Would have saved them a lot of scrubbing."

"Them?"

"Of course them. They made a mess, they cleaned it up. Now, my grandchildren," she added, "they've never cleaned up after themselves in their lives."

She got a funny look on her face then. Like she was going to hurl, maybe. But ghosts don't hurl. Unless they hurl ghost puke, Pen insists on adding.

"Goodness," Franny said without hurling ghost puke. "That's odd."

"What is?" Theo asked.

"I can't remember their names. My grandkids' names."

"Well," said Theo, "you haven't seen them in a while."

"True," said Franny. "But I'm sure I remembered their names when I got here." She frowned. "This isn't good," she went on. "I feel like I'm losing my memories from after I lived here. And on top of that, I had an urge to do some filing earlier. I always hated filing."

Denny told the others about the weeding incident, which reminded us of Theo and the sword.

"We seem to be reverting to our child selves," said Franny. "Which might explain that silly spat between you and Charlie the other day," she said to Denny.

Denny muttered something.

"What did you say?" Franny asked.

"I said that Charlie thinks he's the gnat's elbows," he muttered a bit louder.

"Which proves my point," said Franny.

"If we revert to our young selves and forget everything else," said Theo, "won't we be stuck here forever? Even if Greta agreed to let us go, where *could* we go then?"

"I don't want to be stuck here forever," said Franny.

"I don't want to be the ghost of a ten-year-old orphan *anywhere*," said Denny.

"Even an island paradise?" Pen asked. "With swaying palm trees?"

"No! Look at these shoes," said Denny. "I hate these shoes."

"At least yours are the right size," Franny grumped.

"Plus, they're all wrong for the beach," said Pen.

"We've got to get out of here," said Denny. "Soon."

28

"OKAY, OKAY," I SAID.

"Okay, what?" Jasper asked.

"Okay, I'll talk to Greta again."

Figuring out what she wanted was the only way to free the ghosts before they were stuck here with only their bad memories, reenacting their orphan chores. We guessed. None of us knew how this stuff really worked. Pen says even someone with a PhD in Ghostology (not a thing) would have been baffled at this point.

"We'll go with you," said Jasper. As if not going with me was ever an option.

"Be polite this time," said Pen.

"I was polite last time."

"Whatever you say."

"The rest of us will stay outside," said Franny. "Maybe it was us being there that set her off and not the rudeness."

"There was no rudeness," I objected.

"Call if you need help," Franny said.

We strapped on our helmets and pads and crept back inside, into the office. I put a nice new green crayon on the desk, and we stood back.

"Why that particular crayon?" Jasper asked, mainly out of nerves.

"Green is soothing," I said. "It's been proven scientifically."

"Good call," said Pen. "Plus, my sisters like the new ones best. I have a really good feeling about this crayon choice."

I waited for the soothingness of the green crayon to take effect, but it wasn't working on me. I felt like I was next up for an oral report I had stayed up all night not writing.

"Go on," said Pen when we'd been standing around for too long in his opinion.

"All right, all right, keep your shirt on," I whispered. "Ah, Greta?" I said in a louder but still very calm and polite voice.

I'd been giving my last attempt some thought and had decided to avoid using her last name. Maybe she didn't like it. Who would?

"Greta," I repeated calmly, "we would really like to ask you some questions. You can use this nice new green crayon to answer them. And this nice sheet of paper. Would that be okay?"

We waited for a response.

"Take your time," I said. "No rush. We'd just like to, um, get your opinion on some stuff. That's all." No green crayon had ever been as soothing as my voice was as I said this.

We waited.

Pen nudged my shoulder when we'd waited long enough in his opinion. "More," he whispered.

"More what?"

"I don't know—flattery, maybe? That works on Cam and Cady."

"Greta?" I said. "We really liked the writing you did on the walls. We totally get where that was coming from. Plus, we loved the drawing you did on the paintings. You made some real improvements."

We waited again.

And then we heard a noise. We were particularly wary of the sound of any cutlery coming toward us, but it wasn't that kind of noise. It was like a tiny sigh. A mouse sigh, coming from just outside the room. It was so small it could have been nothing.

"Greta?" I whispered, kind of hoping it was nothing.

Or even a mouse. "Is that you? You can come in. We won't bother you. We want to help."

The mouse or possibly the poltergeist but definitely not nothing sighed again, a little louder. And then Greta came into the room.

29

ALL THREE OF US KNEW THE moment she arrived. We compared notes afterward. How did we know? That we aren't so sure about. Something about the atmosphere in the room changed—the way it would if you opened a window in a stuffy room on a fresh day. Or vice versa.

Also, you know that expression that everyone uses about the hairs on the back of your neck standing up? That actually happened. Not to me or Pen; the hair on the back of our necks is too long to stand up (or lie down properly, if you ask the mothers). But Jasper says his did. He says it's really a matter of getting goose bumps on the back of your neck, which makes the hairs there (if they are short enough) stand up. Like the hairs on our arms were doing. None of us noticed what was going on with the hair on our legs at the time.

Pen and Jasper have advised me to get on with the story or they will close the laptop on my hands. So. We were already standing well away from the desk, but we all wished we weren't frozen in place by fear and could move even farther away as Greta approached.

We could tell she was approaching even though we couldn't see her and she wasn't making any noise. When she moved, dust started to swirl around—we could see it in the sunbeams coming through the windows. And there was a slight ripple in the air. Imagine that there's a piece of clear plastic stretched in front of you so smoothly that you can't see it, and then someone taps on it. That's kind of what it looked like.

We knew she was capable of making shrieking sounds and blowing around like a whirlwind and freezing us, so the only explanation we can come up with for this subtlety is that she was being *careful*.

As we watched, some of us with our mouths gaping, the green crayon moved on the desk. It shifted a few inches. Then it rose into the air and made a few wobbly spirals. Then it dove down toward the paper, hit it, and started to write.

Jasper swears the hair on the back of his neck may never lie down again. Yes, we had been shrieked at and chased by this thing; it had thrown bric-a-brac at us and tried to chop us up or maybe stab us. All of which had been terrifying. But standing still and watching the same entity slowly move a crayon across a sheet of paper was worse. Possibly because we couldn't let off steam by running away screaming.

Her control over the crayon wasn't great, and her letters were shaky, like yours would be if you were writing with your other hand. The first thing she wrote was, and it didn't come as a surprise to any of us: "MINE."

The crayon fell on its side and lay there not moving when the word was complete.

Pen nudged me.

"Ah," I said, my mouth completely dry and my tongue curled up in there like a withered leaf. "Do you mean this house, Greta? This house is yours?"

The crayon righted itself and began writing again.

"ALL MINE." (I'm putting periods and quotation marks in here to make things clear, but she didn't include them.)

"Okaaay," I said. "It's all yours. I don't think anyone here would disagree with that. Would we, guys?"

The guys glared at me, horrified at having been dragged into the "conversation." They shook their heads.

"Um," I said, "is there anything else you want to add to that?"

"GRETAS" came next, slightly more quickly than the other two, as if she was getting better with practice.

And here's where Pen lost it.

He admits that he lost it. He claims he was starting to have to pee and ran out of patience. "Yes," he said loudly when she'd dropped the crayon again, "we get it: This whole awesome place is yours. Now can you maybe tell us why you're keeping the other orphans here when they clearly have places they'd rather be? And can you maybe use full sentences, or at least a couple of verbs? And what about apostrophes? Ever heard of—"

I was lunging to put my hand over his mouth when the green crayon hit him smack in the eye.

30

"HE'S GOING TO HAVE A BLACK eye," said Franny when we'd gotten Pen outside.

"It's more green right now," said Denny.

He was right. The big green crayon had left a big green smudge under Pen's eye, the eye that would later be purple (and then green again, and then yellow).

"Geez, Pen," I said when it was clear he was basically okay. "Now who's not being polite to the poltergeist?"

"I know," he said. "I'm sorry." He touched the waxy green area under his eye with one finger and winced. "I guess you can't call me 'Pen' anymore," he added.

"Why not?"

"I'm thinking you should probably call me 'Crayon' instead."

"That's not funny, you know."

"I know. I think my brain might be injured."

"I think not," said Franny.

"My personality might have been affected."

"Doesn't seem it," said Denny. "But where's Martha Mump? Wasn't she a doctor?"

"Dr. Mump?" said Pen. "That was her name?"

Theo went off in search of Dr. Mump. In the meantime, Lorna appeared on the porch.

"She's written a whole note," she said. "Come see."

Jasper and Denny and I went back into the office. Pen didn't come with us. He knew he was banned.

There was no sign of Greta when we got to the office, except for the additional writing she'd left behind.

Here's what it said, and if you can figure out what she wanted at this point, then you're way better at clues than we were.

ALL GRETAS
FIND HER
BRING GRETA
THEN THEY CAN GO

"Ack!" Jasper whispered. "What's that supposed to mean?"

"I thought *she* was Greta," I said. "What's that about

bringing her? And is that 'GRETAS' meant to be plural or possessive?"

"I see it as rather encouraging, myself," said Denny.

"How?" Jasper and I both asked.

"She's cooperating. She has indicated that we can leave if we 'bring Greta.' This is good news. We've come a long way."

"Really?" said Jasper. "Because I feel like we just lost a big part of the puzzle we thought we had in place. The whole who-she-is part."

"At least whoever she is, she used verbs this time," I said. "Pen will be pleased. I mean, Crayon will be pleased."

Or he would have been pleased if he'd still been there when we got back to the porch with the good-news / mostly-bad-news report.

Dr. Mump had taken a look at his eye, told him his brain wasn't injured and to stop poking at it (his eye, not his brain), and recommended that he go right home and put an ice pack on the swelling. Jasper and I took this as a sign that we should return to the local-history room for more information. About the orphanage, or Greta, or the tribrowed librarian herself. Or even all of the above, if we got lucky.

The library was refreshingly calm after our hair-raising (literally) time at the orphanage. Jasper and I went upstairs to the local-history room. The door was closed.

"Maybe she's at lunch?" said Jasper.

"I don't think so," I said.

"Why? Just because she's got three eyebrows doesn't mean she doesn't eat like a normal person."

"Look at the paper taped beside the door here."

"Oh."

The paper taped beside the door said, in black marker, "Local-history room closed indefinitely. Please consult the reference librarian for details."

The reference librarian was a lot less heebie-jeebie-making than the local-history librarian. She was always perky and energetic and "Let's look it up, shall we?" She didn't act perky when we asked her about the local-history room, though. Her face fell, as the cliché goes.

"I'm sorry," she said. "The library doesn't have enough money to keep the local-history room open. It isn't used enough to make it worthwhile. They closed it yesterday."

"So how can we look stuff up in there?" asked Jasper.

"Today you can't. At some point it will be open by appointment to people who need access to the materials there."

"What if we want to talk to the librarian who worked there?"

Her face fell even further. Down around her neck, almost. "I'm sorry," she said again. "You can't talk to her. Greta was laid off yesterday. She doesn't work here anymore."

31

GRETA? GRETA WAS THE TRIBROWED LOCAL-HISTORY librarian's name?

What, exactly, were the odds of that? Coincidences were popping up like pimples on Neil's chin. Jasper and I discussed this as we practically ran the whole way to Pen's house to tell him.

"Neil doesn't have that many pimples," Jasper tried to claim.

"Not the point, actually," I said. "And yes he does. The point is that maybe the librarian is the Greta we're supposed to find."

"She can't possibly be the Greta who lived at the orphanage."

I did the math in my head. "No, she can't be that

Greta. But she's *a* Greta. And she has three eyebrows. It has to mean something. Doesn't it?"

"Maybe it's a more popular name than we thought," said Pen when we got to his house and told him what we'd heard.

He was lying on the sofa with a bag of frozen corn on his eye.

"Ew," I said when he took the bag off to turn it over.

"I know, I hate corn," said Pen. "But Mom needs the peas for dinner."

"I was talking about the eye, but never mind."

Pen beckoned us both closer and whispered, "I told my mom a baby in a stroller threw a crayon at me as we were walking down the sidewalk. So don't contradict that if it comes up."

"You told her you were attacked by a baby?"

"Not *attacked*. I told her it was an accident. The baby didn't mean any harm. Remember that so you can corroborate: *The baby didn't mean any harm.*"

"Uh-huh. Anyway," I said, "I personally don't think Greta is all that common as a name, and I still don't think three eyebrows are all that common as a facial feature. I think it means something, and so does Jasper. Right, Jasper?"

"I guess," he said.

I ignored his lukewarm response. "So here are the issues as I see them," I said.

"Here we go," said Pen. "Issues incoming."

I ignored his snarky attitude. "The poltergeist, who may or may not be the orphan Greta, wants us to find someone named Greta because the house is hers. Supposedly. Even though we know it belongs to SPEC. Which doesn't exist anymore. And the librarian, who looks like Mrs. G, is named Greta."

"What if the poltergeist *is* Greta and she talks about herself in the third person?" Pen asked, not unreasonably. "Plenty of little kids do that."

"True," said Jasper. "And she also wrote 'Mine' all over the place, don't forget."

I *had* been forgetting that. Then I remembered something else: "She also wrote 'Find Greta,' though. And she couldn't have meant for us to find *her*. She's there. Right?"

"We found *a* Greta," said Pen. "Maybe that's good enough."

"We sort of found her," I said. "But we lost her again. She got fired and now she's gone."

"So let's look her up," said Jasper.

"Without a last name?"

"Pen, can we use your family's computer?" Jasper asked.

"What are you going to do," I asked, "search for all the Gretas who live around here?"

"We could," said Jasper. "But I have something easier in mind."

"What?"

"The library's website. Chances are they haven't taken her name off if she was fired yesterday."

Greta Albert was her full name. Not Grump, but we weren't expecting that. Greta Albert lived in Frog Lake, we learned from googling her. Not too far from the library.

So we had the information we thought we needed. The question was what to do. Could three kids show up at someone's house and demand to know why a poltergeist may have trapped a bunch of ghosts at an abandoned orphanage so they'd help find, possibly, her? Could they also, in a really tactful way, ask her about her third eyebrow?

We couldn't agree on any of these things, so we gave up and spent the rest of the afternoon burying a few bottle caps, a couple bent nails, and two nickels and seven pennies out in the woods by the soccer field, in the rootiest possible spots, for Neil to find with his metal detector.

It wasn't until we'd buried each of these things in its own hole—and we weren't getting much better at digging, and the day wasn't cool—that we remembered there was almost no chance Neil's crummy homemade metal detector actually worked.

I waited the next morning until Neil had left for the woods, then called Pen and Jasper and told them the coast was clear.

My deluded brother hadn't looked nearly as enthusiastic setting off as he had before. No spring in his step today. He looked more like a guy heading to the bus stop on his way to a boring office job. He was getting worn down. I was pleased.

There was more bad news at the orphanage when we got there.

"You need to hear this," said Franny, appearing without even saying hello as soon as we'd reached the porch.

"Okay," we three said at the same time.

"Sally!" Franny called. "Get over here and tell the boys."

A ghost we hadn't met before floated around the corner of the porch and up the steps. She looked like a teenager and she was, even as a ghost, seriously pretty. We all thought so, and we usually have different ideas about what's attractive. She had wavy hair and sparkly eyes and a brilliant smile.

"Hi," she said. "I'm Sally. Sally Sump-Pump." Then she waited.

Pen bit. "Seriously?" he said. "Sump-Pump is your last name?"

Sally laughed. This made her even prettier. The three of us were becoming dazzled by her prettiness, we freely admit.

"That's my married name," she said. "Funny, I know.

That's partly why I did it. I met my husband here. Pete Pump. So it was Sally Sump, Sally Pump, or Sally Sump-Pump. I chose the funniest one."

"Sally?" said Franny.

"Yes, Franny?"

"Tell them."

"Sorry, Franny. As I said," Sally told us, "Pete and I met here. But we didn't get along back then. We argued about everything. It wasn't until we met again after college that we realized we'd been in love the whole time."

"That's so romantic," said Pen.

"Right?" said Sally. "But now . . ." Her sparkly eyes got shimmery. Did ghosts have ghost tears? "Now Pete doesn't remember anything beyond what happened to us here. He's gone back to calling me 'Silly Sally.' He doesn't remember our marriage at all."

"It's another sign," said Franny to us.

"Of what?" I asked.

"Of our need to escape from here before we completely forget every other part of our lives," said Franny.

"We made some progress, we think," said Jasper, trying to stop the downward spiral of gloom. "We found out that the librarian—the one with the three eyebrows? Her name is Greta."

There was silence from Franny. "I'm sorry," she said after a bit. "I'm not sure how that's progress."

"We don't see how it can be a coincidence," I said. Though now, with Franny's skeptical face and Sally's sad one right in front of me, I couldn't say why not. "We're thinking—hoping, anyway—that the librarian Greta might be the one we're supposed to find."

Sally sniffled even though we're fairly certain ghosts don't have snot. Jasper would like to go down on record here as stating that he objects to all past and future references to ghost bodily fluids in this journal. Which Pen and I think is both a shame and a lost opportunity.

"We need to know if this Greta you found is the one we want, then," Sally said. "As soon as possible."

"And how do you propose we find out?" I asked.

"Ask Greta," said Franny.

"How could she know?" Jasper objected.

"Not the librarian," said Franny. "The poltergeist. Now get in there and *be polite*."

32

"SO, AH, WE FOUND A GRETA for you," I called tentatively into the still, dust-mote-filled air of the office. "She's a librarian. Her name is Greta Albert. Is she the Greta you're looking for?"

We waited while nothing stirred the dust motes. ("We" being Jasper and me. Pen was still banned for his own safety.)

"Greta Albert?" I tried again. "Does that name ring any bells for you?"

Jasper gave me a *Ring any bells? Really?* face.

"What if Albert is her married name or something?" I whispered to Jasper, remembering the whole Sump-Pump discussion earlier. What is it with women and last names? Why can't they stick with what they're given like the rest of us? Do I like the idea of being a Pfefferkuchen my whole life? I do not. But I'll manage to live with it.

Jasper held up an *I have an idea* finger. Then he called out: "Her name is Greta, and she has three eyebrows!"

She didn't bother with any theatrical crashing or shrieking sounds or temperature changes. She didn't bother with any bric-a-brac or antique weapons. She just came at us with the full force of her anger. One second she wasn't there, and the next she was all over us.

Way back when we first met him, Theo described how the poltergeist kept them from leaving the grounds of the orphanage. He said the punishment was like being stung by a wall of wasps. Well, that's how it felt for people with no substance.

For Jasper and me, who had plenty of substance, it wasn't a wall. At least a wall has a defined area of not-wall that you can leap away from if you run into it. For us, it felt like we were enveloped in a cloud of enraged wasps—something we already had experience with. But then the cloud closed in around us until we were both wearing tight suits of wasps that included socks and hats—the knit kind that muggers wear with only eye and mouth holes. This was like nothing we'd ever experienced.

The stinging pain was unbelievable. We closed our eyes and screamed.

Pen, who had been pacing nervously out on the porch, charged into the house as soon as he heard our screams, and the ghosts streamed after him. He says he couldn't see anything wrong with us. We were standing in the middle of the office, eyes shut, arms at our sides, screaming.

Pen didn't even try to guess what had happened to Jasper and me. He says his only thought was something like: *How rude could they have been for* this *to happen?*

Jasper was closest, so Pen grabbed him around the waist in some kind of football hold (none of us know how to play tackle football, as you've probably assumed) and plowed him out of the room. Then he went back for me and pushed us both down the hall and out the front door.

The polter-wasps didn't bother Pen. He says he was moving too quickly and doing too many tricky maneuvers for Greta to latch on to him, but Jasper and I disagree. Our theory is that Pen's ghastly eye still seemed like enough punishment, even for her.

Jasper and I also think Pen would make an excellent firefighter. He stormed in there and evacuated us without regard for his own safety. We are forever in his debt. Which we will be paying back in a variety of ways for a long time, believe us.

After Jasper and I had been out of the house for a few minutes and Pen had doused us with water, the stinging pain wore off enough that we were able to speak in halting, gaspy sentences.

"I'm sorry," said Jasper. "It's my fault. . . . I didn't think she'd take it so . . . badly."

"Take what so badly?" asked Franny.

"I mentioned the—"

"Not out loud!" I said.

"The . . ." Jasper pointed to his own two eyebrows and then to the space between them. "You know."

"Why would she be mad about that?" Pen asked.

"She really . . . hates the Gs," I reminded him.

"But we weren't talking about them. . . . We were talking about . . . the librarian," said Jasper.

"Maybe any reminder of the Gs makes her angry," said Theo.

"Maybe."

Jasper and I studied our exposed skin, looking for any sign of what had felt like hundreds of stings. Not even a welt on either of us. Because we were busy studying, we didn't notice at first when the sign appeared. It was Sally who pointed it out.

"I guess she's speaking to you again, anyway," she said.

"Huh?" said Jasper.

"The window," said Sally. "See?"

We did now. A section had been ripped from one of the big pieces of paper we'd left in the office. It had been propped up somehow against the glass, facing out so we could read it. In bold blue crayon, it said:

"BRING HER HERE."

"That seems definitive," said Denny when we'd all taken the two seconds necessary to read the sign.

"Definitive, yes," said Jasper. "But not easy."

"Why not?" said Theo.

"Grown-ups aren't as easy to lure to haunted orphanages as kids are," Pen said.

"Good point," Theo agreed. "It wasn't all that easy to lure you three here, as I remember. And you're gullible."

"We aren't gullible," Pen objected. "We're open-minded. It's a spirit-of-adventure thing with us."

"You're going to have to tell the librarian some version of the truth," said Franny.

"But we're not even sure what the truth is," I said. "We've been calling the poltergeist 'Greta,' but we don't actually know who or what the poltergeist is. Or why it wants the librarian here, or even what it's going to do to her if we bring her. What if it attacks her? It seems to enjoy attacking people."

"We won't let that happen," said Denny. "We'll look out for her the way we did you."

This wasn't as reassuring as he seemed to think it was, but we nodded politely.

"Just get her here," said Franny. "Before we all turn into mindless ghost-husks of our former selves."

"Zombie ghosts," Pen muttered to himself. "Verrry innn-ter-est-ing . . ."

"Go!" said Franny.

So we did.

On the way home, we discussed options other than telling Greta Albert the truth.

"We could tell her she won the lottery, but she has to come to the orphanage to collect the money," said Pen.

"She'd probably know she hadn't entered a weird, abandoned-orphanage-based lottery," said Jasper. "Maybe we could tell her we saw smoke coming from there and wanted an adult to come with us to make sure it wasn't on fire."

"She would have to wonder why we randomly chose her," I said. "I mean, why didn't we call the fire department?"

"Maybe we can't call the fire department because we kept calling and reporting fake fires and now we're forbidden to contact them," Jasper suggested.

Even Pen groaned.

"We need to exploit her weaknesses," I said.

"What weaknesses? We don't even know her."

"She's a librarian. Let's tell her we saw an unreturned library book in the orphanage."

"That's a terrible idea," said Jasper. "But it gives me a better one."

33

JASPER'S IDEA WASN'T GOOD AT ALL, but it was the only one we had that wasn't terrible. So we agreed that the next morning, when Neil had left to go treasure hunting, we would walk to Greta Albert's house and put it into action.

We'll never know if Jasper's plan would have worked, because we didn't end up using it. And you'll never know what it was, because Jasper is ashamed of it and doesn't want to reveal it here. Maybe I'll stick it in as a footnote later.

Jasper informs me that if I stick it in as a footnote, he will stick *his* foot somewhere that I will not be happy to have it. Sorry. You'll just have to wonder.

Before we could even try to put the not-good plan into

action, another problem loomed. It loomed in the doorway of the bathroom that morning as I was brushing my
teeth. Its morning breath was dizzying. And its name, in
case you don't already know, was Neil Pfefferkuchen.

"Whatcha getting ready for so bright and early this
morning?" he asked.

"Nothing."

"Then why are you brushing your teeth?"

"Because I care about good oral hygiene," I said around
my toothbrush.

"No, you don't," he said. Correctly.

"You must have something better to do than watch me
brush my teeth," I said. Incorrectly.

"You and your twerp friends are neck-deep into
something," said Neil. "I know it, and you know it. Our
parents don't know it. *Yet*. But I am watching you, Typo.
And I am like the wind—everywhere and nowhere. Get
my drift?"

This was a lot to take in so early in the morning, with
my mouth full of toothpaste. First, my flea-brained brother
hadn't been totally distracted by the treasure-hunting ruse.
Second, his wind simile was pretty impressive. And third,
his unintentional wind/drift pun was kind of funny.

"Mind your own beeswax," I said. Not my best come-
back, I know. I spat out my toothpaste.

》》X《《

When the three of us got to Greta Albert's house later that morning, we stood around on the front porch like first-time trick-or-treaters, waiting to see who was brave enough to ring the bell. Which none of us was.

After we'd spent a few minutes bickering and shuffling around, the door opened about halfway, and the librarian stood before us, looking cranky and suspicious.

"What are you boys doing on my porch?" she asked.

Put on the spot like that, all I could think to say was that we'd seen smoke coming from the woods and needed her to come with us to investigate. Jasper's slightly less terrible plan had completely left my mind. Before I could say anything, though, she did.

"Are you Frog Scouts? Are you selling Frog Scout cookies?"

This was the second time that summer we'd been accused of being Scouts of some kind. Did we look that wholesome and outdoorsy? We don't think so.

"There's no such thing as Frog Scout cookies," said Pen. "I think they might sell popcorn. Possibly the caramel kind. But it might have nuts, so . . ."

Greta Albert pursed her lips the way some women do when they're irritated. "If you aren't Frog Scouts, then what are you doing here?" she asked again. Her glasses hung on a chain around her neck, and now she put them on, as if to inspect us more carefully.

All three of us took a step back, and I almost fell off the porch.

"Aren't you two those boys from the local-history room at the library?" she asked, eyeing me and Jasper.

This is where Jasper's plan fell apart, since it involved pretending we were something other than "those boys from the local-history room." And you must know by now that if one of us is going to start winging it, it will be Pen.

"That's right," he said, moving in front of Jasper and me. "My esteemed colleagues here were doing some important local-history research, and they didn't quite finish—probably goofing off; you know boys!—and now it's closed. So we were hoping you could help us, since you work there—or you did work there till you were fired. But you still know stuff even if you were fired, right? You weren't fired for not knowing local-history stuff. Were you?" he concluded breathlessly.

Greta looked torn between a tiny tidbit of curiosity and a big chunk of wanting to punch Pen's babbling face.

"I was not fired," she said. "I was laid off. It's different. If you need further help with your project, I suggest you ask the reference librarian. She can make an appointment for you to use the materials in the local-history room. Now, if you don't mind . . ." And she started to close the door.

Pen, thinking quickly but not safely, stuck his head in

the door—practically inviting her to close it on him—and asked, "Are you named after someone?"

"What?" She didn't close the door on his head, but she must have been considering it.

"Is your name Greta because you were named after someone? Another person named Greta?"

"Why would you want to know that?"

Jasper jumped in here, for better or worse. "In our research, we found a person named Greta. Greta Grump. She lived at an orphanage here in Frog Lake when she was little. We were wondering if you know anything about her, since you have the same name."

Greta Albert glared at us. If she'd had any type of laser vision, we would have been incinerated into three little heaps of ash on her front porch and blown into the shrubbery with the next puff of wind.

"Greta is not an uncommon name," she said finally.

"See?" said Pen to me and Jasper. "I told you."

Greta continued to glare for a few excruciating seconds, but then her curiosity got the better of her. She sighed. "I am related to Greta Grump, as she was called when she lived at the orphanage. I'm her granddaughter."

"Jackpot!" said Pen.

"*Excuse* me?" Greta said. She wasn't really asking to be excused, as you know. She was telling us—or Pen, specifically—that we'd been so rude that we needed to be excused, and since we hadn't said it, she would.

"Sorry," said Pen. "It's just that we were hoping there was a connection between you and Greta Grump."

"And why is that?" asked Greta.

"It's a long story," said Jasper.

Which was the most sincere thing any of us had said on that porch, and she must have realized it.

"Then you'd better come in. Wipe your feet first, please."

We wiped our feet and filed into her house, amazed that we'd gotten that far.

We could only hope that she didn't take after her grandmother in the hospitality department.

34

GRETA ALBERT TURNED OUT TO BE nicer inside her house than she was in the doorway. We told her our names, and she told us to have a seat in her living room. Then she went into the kitchen for some lemonade.

We sat quietly and looked around. It was a small living room (it was a small house, so it made sense) with lots of bookcases. And the bookcases were full of books, which many people's bookcases are not, I have noticed. Many people use bookcases for "collectibles," which is a word that seems to mean "other people's yard-sale junk." Of course, lots of people sell their old books at yard sales, so it gets complicated.

Pen and Jasper do not appreciate my attempts to, they

say, "make this journal longer for no good reason." Jasper claims that we could lose a whole grade point for "aimless noodling." So my thoughts on bookcases, books, and collectibles have been cut short. Maybe I'll include them in next year's summer journal, which will not, I repeat *not*, have any coauthors.

Greta brought us each a glass of lemonade, which was, we were sorry to find out, homemade. If anyone ever offers you a glass of homemade lemonade, don't be tempted. Some things are better homemade. These include chocolate-chip cookies and most Halloween costumes. They do not include French fries, bathing suits, or lemonade. Homemade lemonade is sour and gritty, no matter who makes it. It just is.

Needless to say, Pen and Jasper have editorial opinions about my thoughts on homemade things too. We'll reach a compromise about these sections at some point, I'm sure.

Greta got right down to business. "How do you know about Greta Grump?" she asked as we took polite sips of the lemonade and tried not to make ick-sour faces.

This was a hard question to answer. We'd heard about Greta Grump from the ghosts she was keeping prisoner at the abandoned orphanage. That was the truth, and none of us thought it was going to fly with the librarian.

All three of us took another sip of lemonade, to kill time and in hopes that someone else would come up with an answer that didn't sound outright bonkers.

When the silence had gone on for too long and he couldn't stand it anymore, Pen came up with "Jasper's great-grandmother told us about her. She was an orphan there too, a long time ago. Her name was Franny Frump."

Greta studied Jasper carefully and did some math in her head. Then she did that lip-pursing thing again.

"Franny Frump must have died well before you were born," she said finally.

Jasper sighed. Pen took a big gulp of lemonade and started coughing and spluttering. I glanced around, pretending to be interested in the books on the shelves.

"You boys have been inside the orphanage, haven't you?" Greta asked.

"Yes," Jasper said. He cracks immediately under direct questioning.

We all tried to seem suitably ashamed of the lying and the trespassing.

"So you're definitely not Frog Scouts, are you?"

"No," Jasper said.

Greta tapped a fingernail on the arm of her chair. "I've been out there," she said. *Tap tap.* "I wanted to have a look at it myself. But there was all that poison ivy." *Tap tap.* "And the hedge had grown completely over the gate." *Tap*

tap. "How did you get in? If you don't mind my asking."
Tappity-tap.

We didn't mind. We were proud that we'd gotten in.

"It's not poison ivy," said Pen. "We thought it was too, at first, but then we, um, found out that it only looks like poison ivy."

Greta nodded. "So that's one obstacle cleared," she said. "What about the hedge?"

"We, um, found a tunnel. That a wombat must have made. We crawled through it."

As you have probably figured out, if you look up "We, um, found" in the Pen Lie-to-Truth Dictionary, you would see that the definition is "A ghost told us."

"Hmm," said Greta. Now she was gripping both arm-rests instead of tapping. "And you went inside and had a good look around? Good enough to look in the files and find Franny Frump's and Greta Grump's names, anyway?"

This was a handy double question. Handy because if you don't want to answer one part of a double question, you can sometimes get away with answering the other part in a long, drawn-out way so the person doesn't notice that you only answered half of their questions. Politicians do this all the time. Except they usually don't answer either part, come to think of it.

"Yes," I said before Pen or Jasper could get in with a less political response. "We've been inside. The first floor, anyway. There's a lot of dust in there. And a lot of broken bric-a-brac." I was immediately sorry that I'd added that detail, afraid she was going to ask if we broke it, but she didn't care much about bric-a-brac. I should have guessed that from her books-only shelves.

"So everything that the Grauches left is still there?"

A sharp lady, the librarian. She knew quite a bit even if she hadn't been inside the place. It was weird, though, after all our careful training, to hear the Grauche name spoken out loud. The three of us flinched reflexively.

"It looks that way," I said when we'd gotten a grip on ourselves.

"Interesting." Greta drank the last of her homemade lemonade, the part that always has sugar grit from the bottom of the glass. "Do you boys have to be anywhere soon?" she asked. "Because I have some questions for you. And some information, too, if you want it."

35

WE DID WANT IT. AND WE didn't have anywhere to be. So we tried to make ourselves comfortable on Greta Albert's not-quite-big-enough-for-three sofa.

"I'll tell you about Greta Grump first," she said. "And then you can fill me in on anything you know from snooping around the orphanage. No offense."

We nodded. We weren't easily offended. About snooping, anyway.

"Greta Grump was my maternal grandmother," said Greta Albert. "You were right—I was named after her. I'm not sure why. I never got the impression that my parents were very fond of her. She was difficult even on her best days. She died last fall."

(Last fall being when the orphans had found themselves trapped in the orphanage, in case you've forgotten.)

"As you know," Greta continued, "she was brought up in the Grauche orphanage for the first years of her life. She was called 'Greta Grump' by the Grauches, in keeping with their unfortunate naming scheme. You may already be familiar with it, from the files."

We nodded again. We were familiar with it. Just not from the files. It now struck all three of us as a major oversight that we hadn't poked around in the files. Except that we were afraid to spend that much time inside the orphanage, where the files were kept.

"The Grauches drowned in a shipwreck—do you know about that, too?"

"From research at the library," Jasper said.

Greta pursed her lips again, but this time it seemed more approving than irritated. "After the shipwreck," she went on, "the orphanage closed, and the orphans went into foster homes. The people who fostered Greta were named Brewster. They raised her until she was twenty, when she married a soldier in the army, my grandfather. They moved to Texas when he was stationed there. She never came back here. But she never forgot the orphanage or the Grauches."

"Why not?" asked Jasper. "If she was really young when she left, how did she remember them at all?"

"Good question. She probably wouldn't have remembered it except for two things. First, of course, the Brewsters told her as much as they could about where she had come from. So she knew she'd been in the orphanage for a time. Second, though, she went to the orphanage once when she was your age or a bit older. Her foster father was a glazier. Do you know what that is?"

We didn't.

"They make and repair windows. One day Greta's father was called out to the orphanage by the people who owned it—an organization called SPEC." She pronounced it "S-P-E-C," not "speck," the way we did. "They asked him to repair some windows that had been broken in a storm. SPEC never used the building, but they didn't want animals getting in there. Or trespassers." She let that word sit for a moment, and so did we.

"Greta went with him. And while he was repairing the windows, she had a look around. Probably not with any memory of the place—more out of curiosity and boredom." Again, she paused to let these words sink in and ring various bells with us. We shuffled our feet on the carpet, finding the pattern there suddenly hugely interesting.

"Greta saw something inside the orphanage that day that set her on an angry, bitter path."

"What was it?" Pen asked.

"I don't know," said Greta. "She refused to say exactly.

My guess is it was something in the Grauches' files. I'm hoping you can help me figure it out."

"We can try," said Jasper, turning into a Frog Scout on the spot.

Greta nodded. "Good. Whatever she saw that day convinced her of something I have never been able to confirm. It consumed her life in many ways. Toward the end, when she was very old—she lived to be over a hundred—she became agitated and made me promise to prove her claim. So I came here to do that, met my husband through the historical society, and decided to stay. I still don't know if she was correct."

"Correct about what?" Pen asked.

She did seem to be beating around the bush more than necessary. We are not adding anything extra to this section to draw out the suspense. It actually happened this slowly.

"My grandmother insisted that she was the daughter of Pritchard and Ermaline Grauche."

36

"EW," SAID PEN AUTOMATICALLY.

"Indeed," said Greta, not taking offense, though if you think about it, she could have. Pen was ew-ing being related to people who may have been her great-grandparents. "Greta hated the idea that her parents could have treated their own child like any other orphan, even giving her a different last name."

"Though it is similar," I couldn't help but point out. "Grauche—Grump."

"True. I've given that some thought myself. Though I can't for the life of me figure out what would have prevented her parents from acknowledging her, if that's who they were."

"Maybe because they hated kids," said Pen.

"What makes you think they hated kids?" Greta asked. "They did run an orphanage, after all."

Here was another question that seemed to box us into blurting out "A ghost told us."

To Pen's credit, he didn't blurt that out. He blurted this instead: "They left their property to SPEC, which was a society for people who hated kids, and the Grauches were really mean to the orphans and took money that was meant for them and gave it to SPEC."

Greta's already magnified eyes widened. "You got that from reading the files at the orphanage?"

"Some of it we got at the library," I said quickly.

"I work at the library, and I was never able to find out what SPEC was," said Greta.

"The Society for the Prevention of Encounters with Children," Jasper supplied.

"That's straightforward, isn't it?" said Greta.

We nodded, grateful to have moved away from the difficult questions about our sources of information.

"As you already know," Greta said, "the Grauches left everything to SPEC in their will, including the orphanage, its grounds, and all their money. My grandmother never got over this. She thought that everything should have been left to her, as their child. By the end of her life she was obsessed with my proving that she was the rightful heir to the Grauches' property, and that all of it should go to me eventually."

Pen, Jasper, and I were thinking about the same thing now: "MINE," written in big crayon letters all over the walls of the orphanage.

"I've never been able to prove that my grandmother was the Grauches' child," said Greta. "I've never even been able to figure out what SPEC was, although it must be defunct now. I have a feeling you boys know even more about this than you've let on. Am I right?"

She was. We explored the carpet pattern in more depth.

"I want you to take me to the orphanage and show me how to get in. Can you do that?"

We couldn't believe it. We didn't even have to make up a story about a fire or a lost library book. Greta Albert was asking us to take her to the orphanage.

Was it really going to be that easy?

No, it wasn't going to be that easy. Of course it wasn't.

We agreed to take Greta to the orphanage. We agreed to go right away. We had nowhere to be, and since she'd been laid off (which isn't the same thing as being fired), she didn't either.

Greta lived within walking distance of the library, which was within walking distance of the orphanage, so we were walking to the orphanage. We'd gotten almost to the library when the unthinkable happened.

A shiny clean car with a gnome-shaped dent in the back bumper slowed beside us, and the monstrous head of the driver poked out the open window. He grinned hideously at the four of us and yelled, "Hey, Typo, you're in big trouble. Get in the car—now." And he rolled to a stop by the curb.

Neil. Once again, showing up when he wasn't needed or wanted.

"Oh, not now," I moaned.

"You too, Yi and Blaisewell," my gargoyle-faced brother said. "I'm supposed to bring all three of you in for questioning." He laughed, which made his gargoyle face even gargoylier. I was surprised rainwater wasn't spouting out of his stupid laughing mouth.

"Is that your brother?" Greta asked me. "He looks exactly like—"

"I'm sorry," I broke in. "We have an appointment we, um, forgot about. Can we go to the, ah, place tomorrow?"

"Maybe I should go by myself," said Greta.

Which was a problem for a lot of different reasons we couldn't explain with Neil honking the horn for us to hurry up.

"Move it, twerps!" he shouted, ignoring Greta and being super rude to her at the same time.

"Give us one stinking minute, loser!" I shouted back.

"You wouldn't be able to find the opening in the hedge," Jasper told Greta. "It's pretty small, and we've hidden it so people won't, you know, trespass."

"All right," Greta said. "I suppose one more day won't make a difference. Come by my house when you can tomorrow."

"We will," we promised. Then we got into the car.

"So," my vile brother said as he made what was probably an illegal U-turn, "you three messed up big-time. Not too clever, were you, Mr. Toothbrush?" He laughed again. None of us bothered to respond. "Typo told Mom he'd be at Yi's. Yi told his mom he'd be at Blaisewell's, and Blaisewell told his mom he'd be at Typo's. A classically stupid ploy. All it takes is one phone call from any of the three moms to bring down your whole scheme."

He was driving with his wrist over the steering wheel, reeking of confidence and cheap body spray. I was totally going to tell Mom when I got home that he'd been driving without his hands in the three and nine o'clock positions, which he was supposed to do at all times based on the Written Agreement following the Incident with the Swerve and Soda.

"My guess is you'll all be grounded," he blabbed. "Something I look forward to, because you know what, children? While you've been out strolling, I have been searching for *your* buried treasure. Your lies and creepy holograms can't keep me away. And you know what else? I think I've just about found it."

You should admire us for what we did next. We were wigged out at the idea that the mothers knew we'd lied this morning. And by the fact that Neil seemed to believe we were capable of making holograms. Did he suddenly think we were some kind of kid geniuses? But we put that aside and did what we had to do: which was pretend we were shocked and horrified to hear that Neil had been going after "our" buried treasure. It was a performance for the ages, and by the end, he seemed sure he'd won not only this round but the whole game.

37

IN ORDER FOR YOU TO UNDERSTAND what happened in the car after we'd dropped Pen and Jasper off at their houses, I need to give you some background information about me and Neil. Jasper has made his opinion on background information clear, but I've managed to get Pen on my side and outvote Jasper by promising that Pen could add an index to our journal. (He's positive he'll get extra credit for it.) See? I am a good negotiator. Want proof? Check under "negotiator, good" in Pen's index.

Okay. I'll try to keep it short. Neil is five years older than I am, which means we were never really buddies. In fact, our parents often put him in charge of me in ways neither of us appreciated. When I started elementary school, he was supposed to walk with me both ways. Which he did—sort of. He would walk about ten paces ahead of me, with some neighbors his age, while I trailed behind them, alone. Who knows what would have happened if I'd fallen or been beamed into a UFO. Neil wouldn't have noticed.

One day in third grade, I went on a school field trip, and the bus came back late. It was raining, and I didn't have an umbrella or a raincoat. Neil, who was in middle school by then, was supposed to walk me home that day, but when I got off the bus, he was nowhere to be seen. Pen's dad offered me a ride, but I said no, Neil would be there any minute. He was not.

I walked out of the school parking lot, which wasn't smart, because the teachers didn't know I hadn't been picked up. They went home. I stood out there on the sidewalk in the rain for what felt like days. Finally, my mother drove up. I hadn't cried yet, but I did when I saw her frantic face.

Two traditions began that night at the Pfefferkuchen house. The first was the use of Written Agreements between Neil and my parents. And boy, was that first one a doozy. There was a separate Written Apology from Neil to Aldo that we both had to sign. The second tradition was my List of Grievances Against Neil. About five minutes into writing it, I got frustrated. I went downstairs, grabbed the thesaurus from the den, brought it up to my room, and looked up "ugly." That page remains bookmarked to this day.

Now, in the car alone with my ogre-spawn brother, I let him have it.

"Why is it," I said, "that you always manage to turn up when I least want to see you, but you're never around when you're supposed to be? Huh?"

"What are you blathering about, Typo?" he said. "Do you think I enjoy being sent to corral you and your little band of twerps when I have stuff to do?"

"What stuff? You sit around playing bad versions of Lord Lawnchair songs on your guitar all day. At least *I* have friends."

"My friends are at work," said Neil.

His doofus friends Eric and Derrick—or maybe Errick and Deric—were both working at Billy Buster's for the summer. Neil hadn't gotten his application in by the deadline. Of course.

"Which leaves you with plenty of time to drive me and Pen and Jasper to the lake. But do you? Oh no. You're too busy threatening to be the wind and following us all over town like a creeper. We saw you in the *library*!"

"That makes no sense," said Neil. "Make up your mind. Do you want me around or not?"

"I want you around when I *need* you around," I said.

I know, I know. Even typing this, I realize I was on thin ice—and no guy with a ladder in sight. But I wasn't quite done. "I wanted you around in first grade, walking to school. But you always ditched me. I wanted you around after the science museum trip, and where were you then? Playing video games, it turned out."

Neil pulled the car over to the curb and put it in park.

"What are you doing?" Was he going to force me out of the car and peel away? Force me out of the car and toss me headfirst into a shrub?

But he only looked over at me. "I should have known," he said. "It all goes back a ways, doesn't it? Still nursing that grudge, are we? How many times do I have to apologize for one stupid mistake? There was a Written Apology, don't forget. I worked hard on that thing. And you signed it!"

"I wrote 'Adlo,'" I said.

"What?"

"I wrote my name wrong. It wasn't official. I never accepted your apology."

38

NEIL AND I WEREN'T SPEAKING BY the time we got home. But that ended up being the least of my worries.

Before we go into what the parents called "the Repercussions," Pen, Jasper, and I want to set something straight. You are probably questioning our intelligence on the lying-about-where-we-were-going issue, and rightly so.

The circular lie (I'm going to his house, he's going to my house, getting ever more complicated the more people there are) almost never works even if your parents don't know each other. But our parents did know each other. In fact, the mothers had really bonded during the urgent care visit. So they knew none of us was where we had said we would be even before we got to where we hadn't said we'd be. (Pen and Jasper hate that sentence and think it's going to send our journal plummeting into C-minus territory. I, on the other hand, know that the best teachers appreciate linguistic complexity.)

Why did we resort to the circular lie when we'd been so careful up to this point? We're embarrassed to say it was an oversight. We'd been so involved in coming up with our plan to get Greta Albert to the orphanage that we hadn't bothered to agree on what we would tell our parents. So each of us winged it. We didn't mean to use the circular lie; it just ended up that way. We are ashamed of ourselves.

End result? Depended on the parents. Jasper was forbidden electronics for two days. Boo-hoo. I was grounded *and* banned from electronics for two days as part of a Written Agreement Regarding Locational Lying. Pen was grounded for three days, during which time he could not use electronics *and* he had to entertain Cam and Cady for two hours each morning. He might as well have been assigned to sweep hot ashes in a netherworld pit—his sisters were into glitter crafts.

But I was the only one who was grilled. And that is because my stinking brother provided details.

"Aldo," said my dad, "why were you wandering around town with a strange woman?"

"What strange woman?"

"Neil said that when he found you, you were walking with a woman."

"He did? Maybe we were passing a woman when he saw us, but—"

My father's face turned stony. It radiated *Don't mess with me when you're already in deep trouble.* "Aldo."

"Okay. It was the librarian from the local-history room, not a strange woman." (Although technically she wasn't the local-history-room librarian anymore, and she was kind of strange.)

"The one with the glasses?"

"Yes."

"What were you doing with her?"

"Um, talking about local history."

"Why?"

"Because it's interesting."

"Since when?"

I didn't bother to answer that. It was more of a remark than a question.

"So are you . . . friendly with her?" my dad asked.

"Sure. She's nice."

Another lie. That's how it happens with lies. Even one tiny one can lead to a cascade of others, to the point where a simple fib about why you're late getting home from school turns into a saga involving alien motherships and creatures with suction cups for hands and parasitic young.

Fortunately for me and my ballooning lie, my dad's phone rang. It was my grandmother, so I knew it would be a long conversation. My grandmother usually slipped me cash when we saw her, but next time, I was going to slip her some. I owed her. As Dad sat down and put up his feet, I ran upstairs to my room and started typing.

39

EVEN THOUGH TWO OF US WERE grounded, we could talk on the phone (landline only). Somehow that didn't count as electronics to any of the parents. Since Jasper was the only one free to move about on his own, he went to Greta Albert's house on the first day of the grounding and asked her to please wait until we could go to the orphanage together. There was no way Pen and I were going to let him go alone with her. What if something interesting happened? Something interesting was bound to happen! She agreed to that, which was patient of her.

I, in the meantime, did a lot of typing, bringing our journal up to date. It was nice to be able to use whatever words and expressions I wanted without Pen and Jasper hanging over me and criticizing. I knew they'd read it later, but by then there would be so much to object to that they'd have to pick and choose. You can decide whether you think they succeeded in reining me in.

We had a long argument, when they read this part, about whether the word is "reining" (which it is), "reigning" (Jasper), or "raining" (Pen, just trying to make trouble). No wonder not many books are written by three authors. Or maybe they are, but none of them are finished yet because of pointless delays like this.

When the endless grounding finally ended, we made careful, non-circular-lie plans to visit the orphanage one last time before bringing Greta. Neil-the-unseen-but-noxious-wind was off somewhere in the car when I left the house that morning, which was convenient. I got the third degree from my mom about where I was going and with whom. (Yes, she uses the word "whom" even though no one else does because they're normal.) Pen and Jasper went through the same thing except without any "whom"s. For the record, we said we were going to the library. Which we did: We met there and then went directly to the orphanage.

Where things were bad. As soon as we got to the front porch, Franny appeared, hands on hips. "Where have you been?" she demanded. "There's a lot of work to do around here, you know! That laundry isn't going to wash itself!"

"It's us, Franny," Jasper said. "We're here to help you get away, remember?"

Franny looked at us blankly for a second, then pulled herself together. "I'm sorry," she said. "I keep losing myself in the past. We all do. Except Stella, naturally."

There was nothing natural about this situation, but we let that slide.

Franny told us all the ghosts were forgetting more and more from their lives after the orphanage: jobs, spouses, kids, pets, and other important things. Several of them now spent most of the day mindlessly reenacting their old orphanage chores. "Poor Clancy," Franny told us, "has been down in the cellar trying to shovel coal."

As we sat on the porch talking with Franny, Denny zoomed around the corner of the house, Charlie right on his heels.

"You're a wet sock, Charlie Chump!" Denny yelled.

"Yeah? Well, you're a crumb, Denny Dump! A wet crumb! A soggy wet crumb!" was Charlie's equally old-timey retort.

Denny whirled around at this, charged Charlie, and tried (we think) to bite his ear.

"Look at us," said Franny mournfully when Charlie had sped away with Denny chasing him and yelling about gnats' elbows. "Look what we're turning into. Sally's moved into the garden shed," she continued. "To get away from Pete. Her own husband." Franny fished around in her ghost apron pocket for a ghost hanky. She dabbed at her eyes.

"We'll bring Greta the librarian tomorrow," I promised. "Tell everyone to hang on for one more day."

"I will," said Franny. "Thank you. And now I'd better get back to sorting the mail."

"That was depressing," said Jasper as we headed back through the woods toward the library.

"No kidding," said Pen. "All that drama and fighting! Tweens can be so immature."

We were almost out of the woods near the stream when I saw a suspicious flash of purple near the edge of the library parking lot. It scurried like a big purple rat behind a dumpster, but then I saw it again, darting behind a parked car. A parked car with a familiar gnome-shaped dent in the bumper.

"Guys," I said. "We're not alone."

40

"**WHAT DO YOU MEAN, WE'RE NOT** alone?" said Jasper. "Don't go all ominous on us, Aldo. Now is not the time."

"Neil is lurking in the library parking lot," I said.

"*Lurking* lurking or just, like, picking up a book?" Pen asked.

"What do you think?"

"What's he doing here?"

"Following us. You heard him the other day. He thinks we actually found buried treasure and made a ghost hologram to keep people away from it."

"A ghost hologram would be a totally cool way to scare people off our treasure," said Pen.

"Until some meddling kids and their dog, Scooby-Doo, discovered us," said Jasper.

"Huh?" said Pen. (No cartoons, remember?)

As we arrived at the parking lot, Neil remained crouched behind our car.

"Neil Pfefferkuchen!" I yelled. "We can see you!"

He stood up casually, like he'd been down there checking the tire pressure or something. He was wearing his Frog Lake High baseball cap pulled low in a lazy attempt at a disguise.

"We know it's you," I said as we got closer. "Maybe you should have worn a trench coat instead of a Lord Lawnchair T-shirt."

But my oafish brother only smiled. It was a smile that said something like *You didn't catch me, twerps. I caught you.*

He rested an arm on the roof of the car. "Where've you been?" he asked.

"At the library, doofus."

"This doesn't look like the library to me," he said.

"It's library property," Jasper pointed out. Brilliantly, Pen and I agree.

Neil had pulled a tiny notebook and a pen out of his pocket and was writing. "Suspects found outside confines of library," he muttered. "Contrary to their stated intentions."

"What. Are. You. Doing?" I asked Harriet the (terrible) Spy.

"I'm working," he said. He finished writing and tucked

the notebook back into his pocket. Where it would later go through the laundry, I was positive. "I've been hired by certain interested parties to keep an eye on you." He tapped the pen against his chin.

"Mom and Dad are *paying* you to spy on me?" I asked.

"They are indeed. It seems you can't be relied on to be where you say you're going to be, Typo." Which was rich coming from him. "And that was before I submit today's report."

"That's . . . such a . . . a breach of trust," I sputtered.

"Dude," said Jasper. "Your own parents hired a snitch."

"Oh, don't be so quick to judge, Yi," said Neil. "I've offered my services to your parents and Blaisewell's. And they were happy to hire me. Tripling my wage." He tapped the pen against his big stupid head. "Clever, no?"

We walked home while Neil tried to tail us slowly in the car. Fortunately for us, an impatient truck driver behind him hit the horn, and he had to speed up. As he passed us, he waved.

"Are we going to get grounded again?" Pen asked. "I can't take any more glitter. It's in my crevices, and I don't think it's coming out!"

"That traitorous chucklehead has no proof we ever left library property," I said. "We'll tell the parents we were taking a break out by the stream. Getting some air."

"What if he has pictures?" Jasper said.

"His phone is never charged," I said, trying to reassure us all. "And anyway, no matter what, even if we have to break out of our locked rooms, we're taking Greta to the orphanage tomorrow, right?"

"My room doesn't lock," said Pen.

None of our rooms locked, but that wasn't the point.

"We're going," I said. "No matter what."

41

THE STRANGE THING WAS, NEIL DIDN'T say anything to the parents about our having left the library. As the two of us sat down to dinner that night, he leaned over and hissed at me: "You didn't see me, and I didn't see you. Got it?"

The parents must have told him not to tell us they'd hired him to spy. Which he had. So maybe we were even? It was getting so complicated to keep track of who had leverage.

"Um, okay," I said.

Then I had to pretend to the spy-hiring parents that everything was normal. The whole situation made conversation so stressful I went to bed early.

≫≫×≪≪

The next day, Pen, Jasper, and I told our parents we were going downtown, to Billy Buster's and then the bookstore. We did stop at Billy Buster's, mainly because we wanted at least some part of our story to be true, and partly because why not have ice cream?

There was no sign of Neil as we ate our ice cream on the sidewalk.

We had gotten to the little bottom tips of our cones when Pen spotted the Pfefferkuchen family car halfway down the block. Parked right in front of the bookstore. With Neil in the driver's seat. How had he snagged that spot? Parking was tight downtown, as my dad never failed to point out.

So now we had to be seen entering the bookstore.

"Here's where we lose him," said Jasper when we were inside.

"How?" I said. "He's got eyes on the door."

"What about disguises?" said Pen. "There's got to be something in here we can use."

There wasn't, as anyone who's been in a self-respecting bookstore knows.

"You say Neil's not exactly a book lover, right?" said Jasper.

"To put it mildly."

"Which means he probably doesn't spend much time here."

"So?"

"So he's probably never had to use the bathroom."

"And . . . ?"

"And he won't know about the back door." Jasper crossed his arms in triumph.

"Genius!" I said. "Right, Pen?"

Pen had his nose in a thick book. "One sec . . . ," he said. "This is the new R. R. Knight. Look at the size of this thing!"

"You can come back for that later," I said.

Pen looked up. "Right," he said. "We've got a polter-ghost problem to solve first."

There was no sign of Neil as we sneaked out the back door of the bookstore and darted from parked car to parked car through the parking lot behind it.

There was no sign of him as we darted from tree to tree on the way to Greta Albert's house.

There was no sign of him as we rang Greta Albert's doorbell at exactly two o'clock, the time she and Jasper had agreed on.

"Looks like we lost him," I said as we waited on the porch.

"We were impressively stealthy," said Pen.

Greta came to the door in some kind of safari getup: khaki pants with lots of carabiners and pockets all over them, a matching shirt-jacket thing with huge patch pockets, and a brimmed hat with a drawstring.

"Um," said Pen, "the orphanage is over by the library, not in, like, the rain forest of Borneo or anything."

"I want to be prepared if I'm going to be crawling through hedges," she said. "And don't be snide, young man. You yourself have glitter in your hair, and you don't hear me making comments."

Pen swiped angrily at the lingering evidence of his crafting with the twins.

Greta put on an enormous pair of dark glasses, the kind that people wear when they've had eye surgery and can't let any particle of light hit their eyes, over her other glasses. Then she locked the door to her house, put the keys in one of her many pockets, and said, "Lead the way."

Now was the time, we had agreed in advance, to tell Greta what to expect at the orphanage. The problem was, we didn't know what to expect. The ghosts had promised that they would hide when we got there so as not to scare Greta immediately. But we still had to worry about Greta Sr., who hadn't made any promises.

"So," said Pen, who'd already been accused of being snide and had the least to lose, "do you believe in ghosts at all, Ms. Albert? Or hauntings in general?"

"Why do you ask?" she replied. Her voice was neutral, and her expression was unreadable behind the medical-grade sunglasses.

"Just making conversation," said Pen, trying to kick a pebble casually and sort of tripping over it.

"Then I would have to say I'm skeptical," said Greta.

"But you wouldn't totally rule it out," said Jasper.

"It's hard to totally rule anything out, isn't it?" Greta said. Which seemed fairly wise, but she was a librarian, after all. They are known for that.

"Especially if you can't explain something any other way," I said.

"Especially then," she said. She removed her sunglasses and squinted at us. "We aren't 'just making conversation,' are we?"

"Well," said Pen, "we are and we aren't."

"Meaning?"

"We are making conversation," he said. "But we aren't *just* making it."

"I see." She put the sunglasses back on. "Do you boys think the orphanage is haunted?"

It was such a blunt question, none of us could resist automatically answering. Which means none of us put any thought into our answers and we all spoke at once.

Me: "Why don't we let you be the judge of that?"

Jasper: "We haven't been able to totally rule it out."

Pen: "Oh, we *know* it is."

As we've already established, Greta Albert was no fool. She ignored Jasper and Aldo and homed in on Pen's bald statement.

"And do you believe it is haunted by my grandmother?" she asked.

This time, none of us answered right away. She looked at Pen and only Pen for what felt like a really long time, even to me and Jasper, who weren't getting looked at. Pen caved.

"Yeah," he said. "That's our theory, anyway."

Greta laughed, or possibly cleared her throat. Then she started walking again, so we did too.

"Well," she said when we'd gone a ways in silence, "if anyone's capable of haunting that place, it's my grandmother."

42

MAYBE IT WAS THE OPEN-MINDED WAY Greta had said that her grandmother could be haunting the orphanage. Maybe it was the dark glasses that made eye contact impossible. Maybe it was the fact that we were getting near the orphanage. Whatever. All three of us started talking fast then: about the original appearance of Theo near the soccer field. About the attacks on us. About the differences between poltergeists and traditional ghosts and memory ghosts. About the way we'd been communicating with Greta Sr. via crayons. About the orphan ghosts getting stuck there, maybe forever.

Greta walked and nodded, nodded and walked, as we made our way behind the library and through the woods.

We don't remember her saying anything after "my grand-mother." It's possible she did and we didn't notice due to our three-way case of verbal diarrhea. Which lasted right up until we got to the new opening in the hedge.

"Here we are," said Jasper.

"Where?" Greta said.

"At the hedge," said Pen.

"I can see that. Where do we go through?" said Greta.

"We just need to move some of these camouflaging branches," I explained, bending down to do it. "And there you have it."

"There *you* have it, maybe," said Greta, peering at the opening. "I'm not so sure *I* have it there." She got down on her hands and knees, took off her Man-with-the-Yellow-Hat hat, and poked her head into the passageway. Only her head. Because the rest of her didn't fit.

If this were a cartoon, now would be the scene where the three of us tried to push Greta through the opening. That didn't happen, mainly because we had our dignity. Well, Greta had most of it. And also because of the sound that we started to notice. A familiar (to three of us) shrieky sound that was getting closer.

Greta reversed quickly out of the passage, stood up, and said, "What on earth is that god-awful noise?" as the shrieking approached from inside the hedge.

"That may or may not be your poltergeist grandmother,"

Jasper said as we backed away from the hedge and some of us got ready to run without stopping until we got home.

The noise was like a massive buzz saw. Or what the three of us think a massive buzz saw might sound like. We don't know. They don't have shop class at Frog Lake Middle School.

It took a moment for us to realize why it sounded like we think a buzz saw might. The hedge was under attack. The whirlwind was hacking away at the branches of the passage. Hedge needles and dust and chips of wood were flying around.

Finally, the noise wound down and the dust and needles settled. We approached the hedge cautiously.

Greta stooped and poked her head inside the passage again. Which was brave of her. Because what if the buzz sawing had only paused for a rest and then started up again with her head in there?

"Whatever it was, it's been quite helpful," Greta reported from partway inside the hedge. "I think I can squeeze through here now."

And she did.

43

GRETA ALBERT, GRANDDAUGHTER OF GRETA GRUMP, alleged great-granddaughter of Pritchard and Ermaline Grauche, and possible rightful heir to the Grauche Orphanage for Orphans, grunted as she stood up after clearing the hedge.

She was there. We had brought her to the orphanage as the poltergeist (we were pretty sure) wanted us to. Our quest was over. So did a rainbow appear over the dilapidated building? Did birds start to fly around and festoon us with garlands and whatnot? Did the newly freed ghost orphans send up a hearty cheer for their saviors?

No. None of that happened.

What happened was that Greta put her safari hat back

on and started walking toward the orphanage. We followed her.

"What a dump," she remarked as we arrived at the front porch.

We'd gotten used to it by now, but when we saw it through Greta's eyes, it really was a dump. The three of us were embarrassed, as if it were our house and we'd failed to spruce it up for our guest.

She spotted the sign and said, "Orphanage for Orphans?"

We could only shrug and remind ourselves silently that *we* weren't the ones who'd come up with that name.

Greta crossed the creaky, slanting front porch and grabbed the tarnished door handle. She may not have felt it, but we three knew we were being watched by lots of unseen eyes.

"I hope this place doesn't come crashing down around us," Greta said as she opened the door and stepped across the threshold.

The three of us didn't dare make eye contact with her or each other when she mentioned crashing. The poor, unknowing woman had no idea how accurate that could end up being.

"But what the heck?" she continued gamely. "In for a penny, in for a pound. That was one of my grandmother's expressions."

Was this her version of nervous babbling? We think it was.

We followed her inside.

"What a mess," she said as she removed her sunglasses and hat and peered into the parlor. Then she wandered down the hall. "I wish I knew what I was looking for."

"If you're looking for whatever it was that made your grandmother think she was the Grauches' daughter," Jasper said, "you should probably start in the office. That's where the files are."

Pen and I cringed when Jasper said the G-word, but the moment passed and nothing happened.

The three of us sensed the ghosts crowding behind us as we followed Greta to the office. It was like having a cloud of cold mist breathing down your neck. Jasper swears he felt an icy elbow or something jab into his back and then quickly pull away.

All of us, corporeal and non-, piled into the office as Greta was already glancing around.

Her first question: "Did you boys crayon all over the walls?"

This hurt. First we'd been lured here because the ghosts hoped we were hooligans who would burn the place down. Then they'd decided we were too Frog Scoutish for that. And now we were being accused of vandalism—in crayon, no less.

"We're not preschoolers," said Pen. "We would've used spray paint."

This wasn't much of a denial, but oh well.

"Then who *is* responsible for this?" said Greta, her librarian voice coming through loud and clear.

"Your grandmother, we think. I mean, the poltergeist," said Jasper.

"But it looks so childish," Greta objected.

Which hurt again, to be honest, since she'd first thought it was something we did.

"Our theory," said Jasper, "is that the poltergeist is sort of a combination of the grown-woman Greta, who thinks the place belongs to you and wanted us to bring you here, and the little kid she was when she was here. The kid part seems to have trouble controlling her temper. And her handwriting."

"How very complicated," said Greta. But she wasn't really concentrating on any of that now. Her gaze had fallen on the paintings.

"Did she crayon on these, too?" she asked as she went over to get a closer look.

"Yeah," said Pen. "She wrote on Mr. G's forehead, and she colored bangs almost over Mrs. G's three . . . um . . ."

Pen wasn't the only one who found himself wishing a shrieking whirlwind would arrive at this moment to rescue him from his flapping mouth.

"Do you want to look in the files?" Jasper suggested in a squeaky helpful-mouse voice he'd never used before. He scampered over to the nearest cabinet and started yanking on drawers. "Maybe the *G* drawer here would have 'Grump' in it"—*yank, yank*—"and you could see what . . . maybe . . . your grandmother . . . maybe . . ." The *G* drawer wasn't giving an inch.

And Greta wasn't listening to him. "Of course," she said. She was running her fingers over the sloppy brown crayon right above Ermaline Grauche's tribrows. "*This* was what she saw when her father brought her here."

"What?" said Pen. "You think your grandmother saw that painting of a nasty . . ." His foot was in it again. "I'm going to wait in the hall," he said quietly.

"It's all right," said Greta. "I'm getting used to you boys and your complete lack of manners. Mrs. Grauche was a thoroughly unpleasant woman, as this portrait indicates. She also had terrible taste in jewelry, it appears. And I'm aware that there's some minor physical resemblance between us. There's no way you could know this, but she and I and my mother and grandmother share a distinctive trait." She came closer to us, raised a hand, and smoothed the heavy bangs off her forehead for a moment, then let them drop back into place. "We all have three eyebrows. It's very unusual. In fact, I've never met anyone else like us. No wonder my grandmother was convinced she was

Ermaline's daughter. I must say I'm convinced too."

And here it came, the shrieky sound, whirling in from somewhere nearby. Except these shrieks didn't sound angry. Could they have been shrieks of joy?

44

THINGS WERE GOING REALLY WELL. GRETA Albert was convinced;
Greta Grump seemed pleased; the ghosts were probably high-fiving invisibly. But then something unexpected
happened.

There was a huge splashing sound, like a rogue wave
hitting the deck of a boat, but we were nowhere near
the ocean. And then there were two semi-transparent
ghosts in the room. They were adults, not orphans.
These uninvited ghosts were angry, their faces pinched
with rage, and they were wearing old-fashioned dress-up
outfits. But most notably, they were soaking wet. At
least they looked soaking wet. Their hair and clothing were drenched, and water was running off their

hems and onto the floor. Where it dried immediately. The moth-eaten carpet beneath them should have been waterlogged, but it wasn't.

Ghosts don't breathe, as we've already stated, but we're all sure we heard a bunch of horrified ghost gasps from various parts of the room as the strangers firmed up and their details filled in.

Pen, Jasper, and I found ourselves huddling together; we'll admit that. By now we'd gotten used to pleasant, dry ghosts and even tantrumming poltergeists, but these angry, wet ghosts were new and horrifying. Greta Albert, who wasn't used to ghosts of any kind, clapped a hand over her mouth and backed away until she was between the two desks.

One of the ghosts, a tall, gaunt man, who in addition to being wet was wearing a coil of brown seaweed like a hat, pointed a pruny finger at Greta Albert and said, *"None of this is yours."*

The other ghost, a very short woman wearing a kelp scarf, nodded her head in agreement. The squelchy bun squatting on top of it wobbled.

Greta put a hand on a desk to steady herself, which didn't work; her face went ghastly white, her eyes rolled up in her head, and she slumped to the floor. The three of us were jealous that she could check out so easily.

The new ghosts were hovering with their backs to the

vandalized paintings. They were dripping wet and draped with ghost seaweed, as we said, but it was obvious who they were, especially since we had their portraits right there to refer to: Pritchard and Ermaline Grauche. Not live and in person, exactly—more like dead and in spirit. And did we mention angry? So, so angry.

"No one," said Pritchard, again with the finger, pointed at us this time, the only ones left standing, "is getting one penny's worth of our property except the Society. You are all trespassing. Leave at once."

He was shaking with rage, which made his seaweed tendrils bobble, which made him less intimidating than he otherwise would have been. Which gave Pen the opening he needed.

"First of all," Pen said, his voice high-pitched but steady, "there is no Society for the Prevention of Encounters with Children anymore. They're gone. Out of business. *Pfft*. Get it? And second, you're ghosts. Which means you don't have any substance. So how do you plan to make us leave?"

"No Society?" Ermaline said in a trembly little voice, which came as a surprise to us, considering her reputation. She tried to grab her husband's upper arm, but of course her hand went right through it, unintentionally emphasizing Pen's second point.

Which was the one Pritchard was focused on. He

laughed before he spoke, one of those un-fun, despicable-person-triumphing laughs. "We may lack substance alone. But we're not alone," he said. "And I doubt very much you will enjoy the company we've brought."

45

THIS NEXT SCENE IS KIND OF gross, so if you're eating, you might want to finish up and maybe wait half an hour before you continue.

"Darling Ermaline," Pritchard Grauche said to his wife, "I think it's time we showed these trespassers our . . . pet." He stuck two fingers into his mouth and whistled.

He might as well have bellowed, "Release the kraken!" Because this enormous . . . sea creature appeared beside him, rising upward and spreading massive tentacles like it was stretching after a long car ride. Its huge pointy head bobbed toward the ceiling like a helium balloon with a slow leak. Its tentacles could easily have grasped us if it had any substance. I know this because one of them passed through my neck like an icy alien probe. I was so shocked I almost dove for cover underneath Greta Albert there on the floor.

"A giant squid?" Pen said. "Your pet is a giant squid?"

"A giant ghost squid," Jasper corrected.

But we didn't panic. Horrifying as the Grauches' pet giant ghost squid was, it didn't have any more substance than they did.

Until the Grauches merged with it.

Remember the Franken-ghost—when three of the orphans joined to protect us from the poltergeist? Remember our surely A+-deserving description of how scary that was? It was Mr. Rogers compared to this new Grauche-squid monstrosity. Pritchard whistled again, the squid dipped its head obediently, and they stepped inside it. The squid solidified as the three merged, making thumping noises as it bumped into the walls and furniture. We could see the Grauches moving around inside it, guiding it like a hideous submersible.

And they were guiding it, needless to say, toward the three of us.

"Get out of our house!" Pritchard burbled from inside the squid.

We were perfectly willing to leave Greta to her fate and run away. We're not proud to admit that, but we are admitting it. The problem was the Grauche-squid between us and the door. Which, looking back on it, seems like foolish positioning on their part. If they were trying to drive us out of the house, why were they blocking the exit? We'll never know.

So we unwillingly stood our ground as three of the monster's tentacles snaked toward us. Maybe it was planning to strangle the three of us at the same time. Or grab us and whip us around the room like rag dolls. But before it could do either of those things, Greta Grump, who'd been quiet since the arrival of the Grauches, joined the fight—not necessarily on our side, but at least against our common enemy.

A heavy metal paperweight shaped like a terrier flew at the head of the Grauche-squid. The creature wasn't coordinated enough to duck, and it was solid enough to catch the blow on its massive head. It reeled for a second but kept coming. A sharp-looking letter opener repeatedly stabbed the tentacle starting to wrap around Jasper's ankle, and the thing, surprised and annoyed, pulled all eight appendages in long enough for us to duck behind the desks.

It was now that we realized we had forgotten to put on our helmets when we came inside the house.

From behind the desks, we started grabbing things to throw at the Grauche-squid. There was a lot to work with—clunky office supplies and hideous "decor." Our aim wasn't as good as Greta Grump's, but it felt good to be defending ourselves. At one point, Jasper threw a fountain pen like a javelin, and the sharp end hit one of the creature's plate-size eyes and stuck there. So extra points to Jasper—for aim and disgustingness.

In spite of all the action, the battle came to sort of a pause after a while, since the Grauches wanted us to leave but were still between us and the door, which prevented us from leaving. We're not sure how long this would have lasted if the next thing hadn't happened.

Which was that the good-guy ghosts started appearing: Franny, Theo, Denny, Charlie, Sally, Lorna, and a few more we knew and a bunch we didn't. They were everywhere—on the floor alongside us, on the desks and shelves and filing cabinets, hovering near the ceiling.

"Orphans!" said Pritchard Grauche. He said it as if he'd spotted half a bug in his sandwich. "Everywhere," he added, as if he'd spotted a lot more bugs and their bug footprints all over the rest of his lunch.

"Grauches!" said Denny in the same tone of voice exactly, only maybe his bugs were bigger and there was bug poop involved too.

"Bundle up, orphans!" Franny yelled.

For a moment we thought she was telling them to put on winter coats. But that wasn't it. They started combining into ghost-orphan-mutants (I'll call them "GOMs" for ease of typing), three or four in each bunch.

"I'm not bundling up with Charlie," we heard Denny whine.

"Right back atcha, wurp" was Charlie's incomprehensible response.

But as in science class, everyone eventually found a partner, and the GOMs attacked as if they'd been waiting all their lives and a lot of their deaths to do it. They surrounded the squid and started pummeling it like it was a grotesque piñata. We almost lost sight of it beneath their flailing mutant arms and fists.

Pen, Jasper, and I just watched, since anything we threw would likely hit a friend rather than the enemy.

We thought it was almost over. We thought the Grauches and their "pet" would go howling back to their watery grave any minute. But the Grauches weren't howling. They were laughing. We could hear their obnoxious laughter bubbling up like toxic waste from inside the battered squid. (Pen says "battered squid" sounds like a tasty seafood item, and Jasper and I can't disagree.)

The squid shook the GOMs off like a wet dog, and then it attacked them. Its tentacles whipped around faster than any of us could keep track of. It picked up GOMs and threw them at the walls, the floor, the ceiling. Mr. Grauche's portrait was knocked down by a flying GOM.

We knew what we had to do then. We got out from behind the desks, armed with a dictionary (me, appropriately), a stapler (Jasper), and an inkwell (Pen) and started whacking the squid with them.

We fought and we fought hard. But the squid was huge, and it had so many tentacles, and the Grauches were getting better at controlling what it did.

And there we were without even our helmets for protection.

46

IF YOU HAD BEEN STANDING ON the stepladder we'd left outside a window of the Grauche Orphanage for Orphans at that moment, you would have witnessed a heroic battle between three kids, a dead squid, a bunch of mutant ghosts, and a poltergeist—a battle involving lots of flailing tentacles and antique desk accessories.

Okay, put that way, it wasn't exactly heroic.

But if you *had* been outside a window of the office during that unheroic time, you wouldn't have been alone. Standing on the stepladder next to you, probably jostling you to get a better view, would have been my brother, Neil.

We didn't see him out there, obviously. We were busy getting our butts kicked.

He won't say what made him go inside the orphanage instead of recording the scene on his phone to share with the entire internet later. But he did. I'll go ahead and type it: Neil Pfefferkuchen showed up when he was needed. Or maybe a tiny bit after he was needed. But still.

He charged into the office, yelling and swinging his cheesy metal detector at any ghost he could, friend or foe—he didn't know the difference and probably wouldn't have cared. "Back off, freaks," he shouted. "No one beats on my brother and his twerpy friends but me."

The business end of his metal detector flew off early on, but the rest of it, you will recall, was a wooden broom handle. So it was an effective weapon, especially compared to, for example, an inkwell. Plus, Neil had played baseball for years and knew how to swing and connect.

The GOMs separated and flew out of harm's way. The squid came for Neil. He stood there like a pimply Greek hero and swung his broomstick at the creature, saying stuff like "Take that, squid breath!" Every time he made contact, there was a moist squelching noise, which was both icky and satisfying.

The ghosts shouted encouragement and unhelpful advice.

"Get 'em, Aldo's big brother!" Franny yelled.

"You got this!" Theo cried.

"Kick it where it counts!" Denny shouted, as if any of us had any idea where it counted on a squid.

Jasper, Pen, and I kept up the fight from the enemy's rear as best we could.

At one point Neil said to us, "Can't you find something better to hit this thing with?"

When we didn't immediately act, he yelled, "The desk drawers, dimwits! Use the drawers!"

We dropped our office supplies and each pulled out a drawer. They were good and sturdy, and when the corners hit a tentacle, it seemed to really irritate the squid.

But we humans couldn't keep this up forever, and it looked like our supernatural enemy could. We were going to get tired, and then we were probably going to be thrown through the windows by the Grauche-squid.

Except we'd forgotten one thing. One very powerful, very cranky thing. There was a howling noise, and something unseen but enraged tore into the squid. There was a sound like wet Velcro being pulled apart, and the Grauches were yanked out of the squid's interior like wailing kids out of a ball pit.

The Grauches' mouths were open in screams of rage, but no one could hear them over the howling. Then the howling stopped, and the squid was engulfed by something we couldn't see. The monster disappeared bit by bit, squirming and windmilling, like it was being swallowed by an invisible whale. And then it was gone. The Grauches' screams died away, and the two of them gaped at the place where the squid had been.

"Squidsy?" Mrs. Grauche whimpered.

There was no time to make fun of this ridiculous name for a giant ghost squid because something even stranger was happening. Where the squid had been, the outline of a small child began to appear. We say a small child, but that's not right. She was not small. And she kept growing as she came into view. Partially into view, anyway. You know how when both of your eyes are open, each one can see an outline of your nose? The child's outline was like that. It never filled in. By the time the outline was complete, the child's head almost touched the ceiling.

"Couldn't she have done that earlier?" Jasper complained.

The giant child reached down and flicked him like a booger. He landed in a heap a few feet away. "I'm okay!" he croaked.

As this was happening, Neil had scooted over to where Pen and I were standing. "What have you three gotten yourselves into?" he whispered.

"Nothing," I said automatically.

Pen was nodding quickly, though. A blurt was coming, even in the middle of this crisis. "I think what we have here is possibly the first combined polter-ghost ever," he said. "The poltergeist, which was invisible, ate the ghost squid. And now the squid is lunch, and the poltergeist has the combined powers of a ghost *and* a poltergeist. It makes sense."

"No, it doesn't," said Neil for the rest of us, including you.

We watched as Greta Grump the polter-ghost moved toward Greta Albert the librarian, still lying between the desks. Greta G leaned over Greta A. Would she eat her, too?

We could hardly bear to watch.

47

GRETA GRUMP DIDN'T EAT HER GRANDDAUGHTER. She picked her up gently, like she was a favorite Barbie. And set her on the padded bench at the back of the room. Greta A let out a little moan, but she didn't open her eyes. Then the giant Greta G turned to the rest of us.

We froze. She didn't have any facial features, so we had no idea what she was thinking. Was she going to pick us up too? And if she did, would she treat us like Barbie's little brother? Does Barbie have a little brother? Pen says she doesn't, but Ken does, and Ken's little brother's name is Tommy. Would we be Tommys—or more like breadsticks?

We were neither.

Greta Grump strode toward her parents, kicking me

aside like a soggy dog toy as she went. I skidded across the floor, getting the worst carpet burn of my life. When I sat up, Neil was beside me.

"Are you okay?" he asked. He looked genuinely worried.

"Yeah," I said, picking carpet fibers from my legs. (It's better to get them off before the rug burn scabs over, in my experience.)

"The only thing worse than a child," Pritchard Grauche announced as Greta G approached them, "is an overgrown child. What is this abomination?"

Greta Grump's outline planted itself in front of the Grauches, hands on hips, posed like every parent's worst about-to-tantrum nightmare. Then she bellowed her favorite word: "MINE!"

One of the windows cracked.

The Grauches stood their ground, but the trembling of their seaweed tendrils gave them away. They were losing, and they knew it, and it was a pleasure to watch them knowing it.

The orphan ghosts came into view again, hovering high against the walls, watching like eager spectators as their underdog team began to pull ahead.

Finally, Pritchard Grauche spoke, his voice shaking like his tendrils. "Perhaps talking would be a more intelligent solution than brute force," he said.

"Per*haps*," said Denny mockingly, "you should have

thought of that before you sicced your barnacle-butt friend on us."

Denny clearly didn't have the least idea about squid anatomy. The thing didn't have a butt, barnacled or not.

"Per*haps*," said Pritchard, mocking the mocking, "you orphans shouldn't be here at all. This is not your property."

"We don't want to be here, and we're not interested in your moldering property," Franny spat.

"Then why *are* you here?" simpered Ermaline Grauche.

"Because your daughter the poltergeist"—Franny gestured upward at Greta Grump—"won't let us leave until her granddaughter the unconscious librarian inherits the place. Lucky her," Franny added in a mumble.

"We have no daughter," said Ermaline.

Greta Grump stamped her foot, and the entire house shook.

Ermaline's portrait fell from the wall.

Pen, Neil, and I scrabbled away from Greta G like crabs. Jasper took cover under one of the desks.

"Of course you do," snapped Franny. "Are you going to keep pretending someone *gave* you a baby? You went to that 'spa' to have Greta, and then you brought her back and pretended she was an orphan. Which is despicable."

"That's nonsense," said Ermaline. "You can't prove any of that."

"But I can," said a voice from the back of the room.

48

IT WAS GRETA ALBERT. HOW LONG had she been conscious? Not long, judging by the woozy way she sat up on the bench and leaned heavily against the wall behind it.

"My grandmother Greta Grump was your daughter," she said to the Grauches, "and I am your great-granddaughter. And I can prove it."

"I sincerely doubt that," said Pritchard, sniffing a ghost minnow out of his nose.

Greta played her trump card. She stood up, pushed her bangs off her forehead, and gave everyone a good view of her legacy.

Ermaline raised a trembling hand to her own version.

"See?" said Pen triumphantly. "She's got the family tribrows."

Greta Grump turned toward him ominously. "Which are great," he added quickly. "*So* great. I'm envious of them. I really am."

Greta Albert turned toward Pen now. "Exactly how long," she said slowly, "were you boys planning to let me lie on the floor without even checking my pulse? And don't try to claim you did, because you didn't. A woman faints, and you three just step around her as if she isn't there, is that it?" She pulled a full-size water bottle from one of her safari pockets and took a long sip. "What on earth is wrong with children these days?" she asked the room. "Absolutely no common courtesy, no concern for a fellow human being."

"Pritchard," said Ermaline, trying unsuccessfully again to grab his arm. Old habits die hard, we guess. Or old habits don't die at all, even when you do. "Pritchard, I like her. She's attractive and well-spoken."

Greta Grump's outline relaxed. She appeared to clasp her hands in front of her.

"This admirable woman can have the property, as far as I'm concerned," Ermaline continued with a nervous glance up at Greta Grump. "What do you say, Pritchie?"

Pritchie cleared his throat. He rubbed his vast forehead with two bony fingers. He tried to seem thoughtful, as if he was deciding, as if he was ever the one to decide. But we're pretty sure he wasn't. "All right, dear, if you insist."

Ermaline made a kissy face at him. It was almost as gross as the ghost squid.

Greta Grump clapped her cymbal-size hands.

A light fixture fell, almost squashing Pen.

The orphan spectators cheered.

"Greta's birth certificate is hidden inside the paper backing behind my portrait," said Ermaline. She turned to point it out. Which is when she saw it for the first time in a hundred years, lying on the floor next to her husband's.

"Did those dreadful boys do this?" Ermaline asked when she'd had time to digest what had happened to both portraits.

"No!" the dreadful boys said at once.

"They did not," Greta Albert confirmed. "I'm afraid your daughter did that in a fit of temper."

Ermaline frowned, which was interesting to see, what with the third eyebrow. "Greta Grauche!" she yelled. "You did this? To your parents' portraits? You are in a great deal of trouble, young lady!"

There was a delighted shriek from Greta Grump. This was what she'd been waiting for since the day she'd first seen the portraits: acknowledgment.

She may have been trying to hug the Grauches; we aren't sure. She took a giant step toward them, bent down, and caught them up in her vast arms. Droplets of water and shreds of seaweed flew off Pritchard and Ermaline as they were enveloped.

And then all three Grauches were gone.

49

THE ORPHAN GHOSTS RUSHED AT US and tried to hug us. Even Neil was ghost-hugged, but he didn't mind once he got a glimpse of Sally Sump-Pump.

"First of all," we heard her saying to him, "I'm married. And second, I'm a lot older than I look."

A ghost we hadn't seen before—a tall teenage boy with a chin like a fairy-tale prince's—rushed straight through Neil to Sally. Then the ghost enveloped Sally in an embrace that left them GOMed for a long moment. The rest of us looked away to give them some privacy.

"Sweetie Petey," Sally Sump-Pump sighed.

"Sal Gal," Pete Pump sighed.

"Ah, romance," Pen sighed.

"You did it!" Denny said to the three of us.

"We knew you could," said Franny.

"I was the one who found them," Theo reminded everyone.

"Are you free?" Jasper asked the ghosts. "Can you tell?"

"I think we're free," said Franny. "I feel like we can go anytime."

"Um, I'm staying?" said Stella. "The orphanage is my home."

"Of course it is," Franny assured her.

"So this is really goodbye?" I said to the other ghosts. I felt like I'd made a bunch of friends at summer camp and now it was over too soon.

"Looks that way," said Denny without any regret whatsoever in his voice.

"I'll miss you, old sock," said Charlie to Denny.

"I'll miss you too, chum," said Denny. "You really are the gnat's elbows."

"Do you think you can come back and visit sometimes?" Pen asked the ghosts. "I mean, you know, for Stella's sake?"

"Maybe," said Franny.

"But probably not," said Theo.

"No," Franny agreed. "Probably not."

"You three can keep Stella company, though," Theo said. "That is, if Ms. Albert will give you permission."

Greta Albert let out a one-syllable laugh. "This place probably needs to be condemned," she said. "And a birth certificate doesn't solve the legal ownership problems. So I'm thinking we should stay away. At least until I've talked to the town. And a lawyer. And a structural engineer."

"Sorry, Stella," said Pen.

"Oh, there's nothing to be sorry about," said Stella. "I'll come visit you!"

Which was a problem for another time.

Greta thanked the ghosts for their help and apologized for her great-grandmother's behavior. "You let me know if she ever bothers you again," she told them.

And then we said goodbye to Theo and Franny, and Denny and Charlie, and Sally and Pete, and Lorna and Martha, and all the other ghosts. One by one, they went transparent and then winked out like sparks landing on dewy grass.

We three were a little misty when it was over, maybe from the ghosts, maybe not. Think what you want; we don't care.

"We should have asked them where they were going," said Pen. "Out of scientific curiosity."

"I don't think they would have told us," said Jasper.

"My goodness," said Greta Albert when the ghosts had been gone for a few minutes and we were less misty, "that was quite an adventure, wasn't it?"

She was sitting on one of the desks. She still looked pale and clammy.

"Maybe you should go home and lie down," said Jasper.

"Why?" she asked. "Do I look like I've seen a ghost?"

We laughed politely at this proof that some jokes really do get old.

Greta may have looked like she'd seen a ghost, but the rest of us looked like we'd taken one of those cartoon falls from high in a tree and bumped every branch on the way down. Both of Pen's nostrils were bleeding. Jasper's hair swoop was standing straight up, and he was sure he'd sprained his other wrist. Neil's Lord Lawnchair shirt was torn in many places. My knees and shins were raw and coated with carpet fibers.

We left the Grauche Orphanage for Orphans together. Greta closed the door behind us.

Neil had parked the car at the library before following us the rest of the way on foot. So he drove everyone home. No one said much in the car at first. We had a lot to think about.

Finally, Neil came out with "So what, exactly, was that all about?"

We gave him a shortened version of the story. And when we were done, he asked a question that the three of us would have come up with eventually, we're sure.

"How does one woman with a grudge manage to trap a bunch of ghosts *after her death* and make them do her a favor?" he said.

Greta, who was sitting in the passenger seat, cleared her throat. "I've been giving that some thought," she said. "And the best explanation I can come up with is that long-festering anger has immense power. Especially among family members. So much power that my grandmother's anger survived even her death."

Neil whistled between his teeth, which is something I wish I could do. "That's a butt-load of anger," he said.

"I'm down here on the left," said Greta, pointing to her street. Neil parked in front of her house, and she got out of the car. Then she walked around to where I sat in the backseat and tapped on the window. I opened it. She leaned in.

"It was anger that trapped those ghosts in the orphanage," she said. "But it was forgiveness that freed them. Which means that forgiveness has even more power than anger." She leaned out. "It's been quite a day," she said. "You boys probably didn't earn any Frog Scout badges for thoughtfulness, but you certainly earned them for bravery."

"We're not Frog Scouts," Jasper reminded her as she went up her front walk.

>>>X<<<

Pen and Jasper want to end our awesome summer journal here, since that was the end of the polter-ghost problem. I have considered their advice carefully, and I agree with them. They are surprised but pleased. They are also begging me to stop dragging it out and just type "The End" already. So here it is:

The End

50

PEN AND JASPER HAVE GONE HOME now, and I am alone with the (swear word, worse swear word) laptop, still typing. The way I see it is, if they wanted our summer journal to end with that last chapter, it did. In fact, you can stop reading now if you want. The rest is extra credit (teacher humor!).

But I'm guessing you, Ms. Pilcrow, have a longer attention span than Pen and Jasper think you do. So I'm going to take advantage of my solitude and your patience, and type a teensy bit more.

As Neil and I drove home that afternoon after dropping Pen and Jasper off, I took a deep breath and did what I knew I had to do. "Thanks for your help back there," I said.

I braced myself for his scoffing denial that he would ever lift a finger, let alone a broomstick, to help his twerpy brother.

Which didn't come.

"You guys were doing all right on your own," he said. With a straight face. "I just batted cleanup."

"Are you going to rat us out to the parents?" I asked. I could barely remember what Pen, Jasper, and I had said we were doing today, but it definitely wasn't what we'd ended up doing.

"Nah," said Neil. "I was never going to rat on you. I just liked freaking you out and getting paid for it. Besides, the only thing the parents really wanted to know was if you guys were hanging out in the Smart-Mart parking lot. Which you weren't."

All I can say is that older brothers can be as complicated as polter-ghosts sometimes.

"How's the summer journal going?" my dad asked at dinner that night. "I hear the old [swear word, worse swear word] laptop getting quite a workout up there lately."

"He's almost done," said Neil without looking up from his attempt to saw through a vegetable that must have been dropped by a passing asteroid. (Mom called it "romanesco." Look it up and see if you agree with me.)

"Neil's been helping," I said, not untruthfully.

"Wow!" said Mom. "So nice that you two are getting along better." She laughed. "But it's kind of funny."

"What do you mean?" I said.

"I mean that when Wendy Yi asked if you, Pen, and Jasper could write your summer journal together, she told Ms. Pilcrow she was hoping it would help the three of you stop arguing so much."

"Mrs. Yi thought working together would make us quit arguing?" I asked.

We've argued about every word in this journal—and a lot of the punctuation.

"Ridiculous, right?" Mom said. "I told Wendy that arguing was your love language."

Which, gross.

But guess what, Ms. Pilcrow? The experiment failed—there's no argument-ending in this journal.

Except there is, actually. Not for me, Pen, and Jasper. That will never happen. But here's the thing. Over the next few days, I gave serious thought to what Greta Albert had said about families and forgiveness. And it occurred to me that if Greta Grump could forgive her parents for claiming she was an orphan, I could forgive Neil for ditching me on the way to school and leaving me out in the rain. At least he'd never pretended we weren't related.

Then, out of the blue one night, Neil came into my

room with a sheet of paper. "I owe you this," he said, handing it to me.

"What is it?"

"A Written Apology. I'm sorry I used to tell people I didn't know you on the way to school."

"Wait, *what*?" I said. "I thought you were just walking too fast for me."

"I told them you were a weird kid who followed me around."

"And they believed that? I look exactly like you!"

"I know. But in my defense, you were always singing that *Sparkle the Spinosaurus* song. It was annoying and also deeply embarrassing for me."

"Sparkle made some good points about self-esteem!" I said. But now I imagined walking to school being trailed by a first grader singing about "I'm the best, and I'm so cool; I can't wait to get to school," and I knew I would have denied knowing me too.

"Anyway," said Neil. "Here's the apology. I hope you'll sign it."

I did. Then I rummaged around on my desk and handed him a sheet of paper of my own.

"What's this?" he asked.

"The Written Apology from the day of the field trip," I said. I pointed to the signature line. "I crossed out 'Adlo' and wrote 'Aldo.' It's official."

The Last Chapter, I Promise

AND NOW, SINCE SCHOOL'S ABOUT TO start, I need to wrap this up, do a spell check, ignore the grammar check, and print it out. So here's the real, final ending.

Pen, Jasper, and I ran into Greta Albert outside Billy Buster's this afternoon. We chatted a bit, and she told us the town is interested in turning the orphanage into a museum, and that she agreed to be in charge of setting it up. So that's cool.

Then she droned on for a long time about back taxes and zoning, almost putting us to sleep standing up. "The structure needs to be made safe before we can do anything, of course," she said when the lecture was over. "Can you believe there were two rusty swords lying around on the property? Anyway, as soon as that happens, you three can come in and help clean and organize. Maybe your whole troop can pitch in. Make it a project."

"What troop?" I asked.

"Your Frog Scout troop."

"We're not—" Jasper started to say, but he was interrupted.

"That sounds great!" said Pen. "I'm in!"

"You're not—" I started to say, but I was interrupted.

"I joined last week," said Pen. "I'm a Frog Scout now for real!"

Neil and I are going to spend the last weekend of the summer treasure hunting. He spent his spying money on a metal detector that works and doesn't have any broom parts. Before you laugh too hard, you should know that before she left, Sally Sump-Pump told Neil about a rumor that went around the orphanage. The story was that the Grauches didn't trust banks, so they buried a lot of their money somewhere on the orphanage property. Probably outside the fence, according to Sally, according to the rumor, so none of the orphans would find it.

I asked Greta at Billy Buster's if we could search for it, and she said, "Why not?" Then she turned away and coughed. Or maybe laughed. Probably a blob of ice cream going down the wrong pipe.

If Neil and I get any leads with the metal detector, Pen is going to help us dig, and Jasper says he'll supervise (his other wrist is, in fact, sprained). We've gotten good at that this summer.

Will we really find buried treasure in the woods next to the soccer field? Well, Pen and Jasper and I might not agree on much, but the three of us know one thing for sure: Stranger things have happened in these parts.

PEN'S USEFUL INDEX

Ermaline and Pritchard, what kind of names are those, anyway?
extra credit, something a teacher would definitely give a
    student who added an actual index to their summer journal

Frog Scouts, non-cookie sales of
future doctors, amazing imitations of

glitter crafts, lasting remnants of in crevices
going first, odds of always being the one who has to
good and evil ghosts, how to tell the difference

hedges, as open systems
heroic rescues, as performed by Pen Q. Blaisewell,
    future firefighter (or doctor)
holograms, as perfectly reasonable explanations for weird stuff

indexes, not as useful as they could be (except this one)

ladders, occasional handiness of
lake ice, surprising thinness of

negotiator, good. *See* Pfefferkuchen, Aldo (at his insistence)

Pfefferkuchen, Aldo, annoying wordiness of
poltergeists, terrible punctuation of

polter-ghosts, world's foremost expert Pen Q.
    Blaisewell's thoughts on and theories about
popcorn, caramel is good but not if it has nuts

scars, things that result from shovel attacks, not bowling

talking to ghosts, outstanding bravery of
    someone who doesn't mind it
tribrow, really good word that should be in the dictionary

ump, most last names are better off not rhyming with
unprovoked shovel attack, thing that actually
    happened in preschool and left a scar

verbal diarrhea. *See* Pfefferkuchen, Aldo

wasps, surprising anger levels of
whittling, accidents associated with

Yi, Jasper, risky and reckless ideas of

Acknowledgments

More years ago than I care to admit, I was riding in the backseat with two brilliant children who happened to be related to me. They were entertaining themselves by making up a choose-your-own adventure-type story featuring the younger one's main interests at the time: ghosts and Pokémon. It was an engrossing tale, and I was sorry when we reached our destination. Having seen how fun it was to tailor a story to an individual's interests, I decided I would try it myself. Minus the Pokémon, which was way over my head. The end result was *The Polter-Ghost Problem*. So my first thanks go to those two (former) children, whom I will not embarrass by naming here. They know who they are.

Thanks to the ever-supportive gang at McElderry: my editor, Karen Wojtyla, for encouraging Denny's insults and Neil's skulking—and for letting me include an index in a novel just for fun; associate editor Nicole Fiorica, for having all the answers; jacket designer Rebecca Syracuse, for the perfect ghostly aura; jacket illustrator Lisa K. Weber, for indulging me with a china poodle; copyeditor Jen Strada and proofreader Benjamin Spier, for being on their toes when I wasn't on mine; and all the others whose expertise went into bringing my ghosts to life.

Thanks to my marvelous agent, Joan Paquette, for her enthusiasm about un-scary ghosts. Thanks to my wonderful critique partners for their support and suggestions, especially Deborah Kops, who inspired the brotherly reconciliation at the end. Ongoing thanks to Paul Swydan and the friendly booksellers at Silver Unicorn, for giving my books a launchpad and "Local Author" stickers. Endless thanks to the librarians and teachers who have been putting my books into kids' hands and letting me know when they find a friend.

And finally, thanks as always to my amazing family and friends, for cheering me on and for cake.